Lara made it to school in reco... jumped out of her car and ran to the rink doors, hoping that Nick was still waiting. It was already after midnight.

"Nick?" Lara called breathlessly into the darkness. There was no response. The room was pitch black, and she could barely see her hand in front of her face. She carefully began to shuffle across the rink.

"Nick?" she called, a little louder. *Nick must have given up and gone home,* she thought. *Some reporter I am, missing a scoop like this. . . .*

Lara turned around and started walking toward the exit. Suddenly her shoe touched something—something heavy. Lara looked down and saw what it was in the dim reflected light of the Exit sign. She started screaming, screaming as though she would never stop.

Collect all the books in the
Horror High series

#1 Mr. Popularity
#2 Resolved: You're Dead
#3 Heartbreaker
#4 New Kid on the Block
#5 Hard Rock
#6 Sudden Death
#7 Pep Rally
#8 Final Curtain

And don't miss these other
thrillers by **Nicholas Adams**!

I.O.U
Santa Claws
Horrorscope

Available from HarperPaperbacks

HORROR HIGH

Sudden Death

Nicholas Adams

HarperPaperbacks
A Division of HarperCollins*Publishers*

This is a work of fiction. The characters, incidents, and dialogues are products of the author's imagination and are not to be construed as real. Any resemblance to actual events or persons, living or dead, is entirely coincidental.

HarperPaperbacks   *A Division of* HarperCollins*Publishers*
10 East 53rd Street, New York, N.Y. 10022

Copyright © 1991 by Daniel Weiss Associates, Inc.
and Bruce Fretts
Cover art copyright © 1991 by Daniel Weiss Associates, Inc.

All rights reserved. No part of this book may be used or reproduced in any manner whatsoever without written permission of the publisher, except in the case of brief quotations embodied in critical articles and reviews. For information address Daniel Weiss Associates, Inc.
33 West 17th Street, New York, New York 10011.

Produced by Daniel Weiss Associates, Inc.
33 West 17th Street, New York, New York 10011.

First printing: April 1991

Printed in the United States of America

HarperPaperbacks and colophon are trademarks of HarperCollins*Publishers*

10 9 8 7 6 5 4 3

To Megan

Sudden Death

Chapter 1

Eight-year-old Lara Crandall woke up from her nightmare with a start. She opened her eyes but could see nothing. She remembered having fallen asleep on her father's lap as he began the drive home from the Canadian vacation her family had gone on. The winding mountain roads had lulled Lara to sleep, but upon awaking, her traveling companions—her parents, Mr. and Mrs. Owens, their next-door neighbors, and their son Billy—seemed to have vanished into the darkness.

Lara cried out "Daddy!" and sat bolt upright. Then everything began to spin furiously and Lara felt sick to her stomach. An intense white light split the darkness and Lara instinctively flinched back from it. She recognized the headlights of an oncoming car, careening out of control and crossing over the double yellow line into their lane. Everything seemed to wind down into dizzy, soundless slow motion.

The light softened into an eerie, muted glow, and for a split second Lara could see clearly again. Her father sat next to her, confidently gripping the steering wheel. On Lara's other side, her mother patiently worked her knitting needles. In the back seat, Mr. and Mrs. Owens each had an arm around Billy, who was sleeping peacefully between them.

Then a horrible sound shattered the silence— the sound of breaking glass, crushing metal, and snapping human bones. Lara's body was hurled against her father's side. She reached out frantically for her mother, but her slumped figure seemed to be slipping farther and farther away from her.

Lara grasped her mother's neck tightly. Her mother's eyes were closed, and a trickle of blood ran down her neck. Looking out the side window for help, Lara saw a twisted piece of steel hurtling rapidly toward her mother's head. She tried to scream out a warning, but she couldn't force out the sound.

Lara felt the impact of the metal hurtling through the glass and ramming into the side of her mother's head, and she held on with all her strength and closed her eyes. A moment after the jolt, she felt warm liquid pouring down onto her arms. She knew it was her mother's blood.

She turned toward the back seat and opened her eyes. Billy held his small hands over a gaping wound in his father's side, helplessly trying to stop the rivers of blood that were flowing out.

He reached one blood-soaked hand toward Lara, but Lara turned away.

Lara shook her mother by the shoulders, trying to get her to open her eyes again. Her mother's mouth dropped open and blood began to cascade out of it. Lara shook harder, and her mother's head pitched forward, now connected to her body by only one thin strand of flesh. One more violent shake, and the strand snapped. Her mother's head fell into her lap, and the eyes popped open and looked blankly up at her. Lara felt herself about to vomit. She managed to scream, then everything went black again.

Lara woke up screaming. She was in her bed at home, and the covers were tangled and strewn on the floor.

"Daddy!"

Then Dr. Crandall was at her bedside. He knew exactly what was happening; Lara never called him "Daddy" unless she was having another nightmare about the accident.

He sat down on the bed and softly stroked her arm. "Everything's going to be okay, honey," he told her quietly. "Try to calm down."

"Dad, it was horrible. I thought these nightmares were going to go away, but I'm having them more than ever," Lara said through her tears.

Dr. Crandall brushed Lara's sleep-matted brown hair away from her red-rimmed eyes.

"They will go away someday, I promise. You shouldn't forget your mother, Lara, but you do have to let go of her. When you do that, maybe the nightmares will end."

Lara sat silently on the bed. She looked up at her father and noticed how he'd aged. She had noticed it more than once lately. Growing up, Lara had thought her dad was the handsomest man in the world—tall and muscular, with wavy blond hair and piercing blue eyes. But a decade without his wife had taken its toll. His hair was thinning on top and turning gray at the temples, and his once-firm physique had sunken into a lumpy paunch.

Dr. Crandall looked down at his hands. "I've got to get to work. We can talk about this more later if you want. And if you'd like to talk to someone else about your feelings—someone professional, someone impartial—I know people down at the hospital . . ."

Lara knew what he meant. "A shrink? Dad, I'm not crazy. I just have bad dreams, that's all." She shrugged.

"Talking to a psychiatrist doesn't mean you're crazy, Lara," Dr. Crandall said, beginning to lose his patience. "It's almost standard practice now for anyone exposed to a traumatic loss to seek some kind of counseling. Maybe I should have taken you to see someone sooner, before these dreams got out of hand, but . . ."

"Dad, forget about it." Lara shot out of bed

4

and grabbed her robe. "I can handle this myself, okay?"

She went to the bathroom to get ready for school. Dr. Crandall sat alone for a moment, staring at the framed, faded portrait of his wife that Lara kept on the nightstand next to her bed.

At school that day, Lara felt an overwhelming urge to talk to Billy Owens about the accident. She and Billy had stayed friends over the years, despite their differing interests, but she always figured it would be better to leave well enough alone. What could be gained from dredging up their painful past?

But senior year was almost half over, and Lara knew her friendship with Billy would fade after graduation. They'd always gone to the same schools, even after Billy and his mom had to sell their house in the elite neighborhood of Gaspee Farms and move to the less-than-respectable Lower Basin. But there was no way they would end up at the same college. Billy might not even get into college with his grades, and Lara hoped to enter one of the nation's top undergraduate journalism programs.

Now Lara felt the future closing in on both of them. What did Billy remember about the accident? Her own memory of it had become more and more cloudy. Over the years, the horrific images of her nightmares had merged with her actual recollections of what happened. She wondered if Billy ever dreamed about the accident.

She knew it had affected him. His father's death seemed to have sent Billy on a downward spiral of plummeting grades. He'd put a lot of energy into the Boy Scouts, until his grades kept him from reaching Eagle Scout. He had always had sports to keep him out of trouble—a full slate of football, hockey, and wrestling—but though he worked hard at each game, his natural athletic talents seemed limited.

Lara couldn't concentrate during her classes that morning. Even her favorite class, journalism, seemed to drag on forever, and Lara barely paid attention to Mrs. Alexander's lecture about the rights and responsibilities of a reporter. When the teacher called on her to define the difference between slander and libel, Lara drew a blank. She knew the answer—slander is spoken, and libel is printed—but her mind was elsewhere. Luckily James Horton, the sports editor and Lara's best friend in the class, bailed her out, writing the answer in big letters in his notebook and holding it up for her to read.

After class, she waited for James outside the door. "Thanks for the save. I don't know where my mind is today. I'm zoning out in a major way. I definitely owe you one," she said.

"No problem," he said, smiling.

James headed for his next class, and Lara made a beeline for Billy's locker. She'd thought about it long enough. Maybe if she acted casual, Billy wouldn't think she was crazy for wanting to talk about the accident after so long.

Billy didn't show up at his locker right away, and a group of cheerleaders who walked by gave Lara funny looks. She didn't care what the pom-pom crowd thought. There had always been gossip about Lara and Billy at Cresswell. Few people remembered the accident, and everyone wondered how a dumb jock from the Lower Basin and a rich brain from Gaspee Farms could be friends. Lara and Billy had been inseparable playmates as kids, but now everyone always assumed there must be something going on between them.

Kim Marsh broke away from the miniskirt-clad pack and sashayed over to Lara. Kim had been dating Billy on and off for two years. The scoop was that she liked Billy for his body, but he didn't have enough money to keep her spoiled rotten. When his cash supply got low, she dumped him. After giving him a couple of months to save up his money from mowing lawns, Kim would take him back and the cycle would begin again. Lara couldn't understand why Billy didn't see through her, and she despised Kim for the way she treated him.

The feeling was mutual. Kim leaned one hand up against Billy's locker and looked Lara straight in the eye.

"Haven't you heard?" Kim asked with a sneer. "Billy and I are going steady again."

Lara stared back. After a lengthy silence, she fired back a single word: "So?"

"So buzz off. You had your chance. This property is mine," Kim said.

Lara felt like punching her right in the mouth. "You are so weak. I'm not after Billy. We're friends. Do you know what a friend is, Kim? I guess not, knowing the way you treat people. Billy and I have been friends for a long time, and we'll still be friends long after he finally gets tired of your game and dumps you once and for all."

Kim struggled for an adequate comeback. "You wish!"

Lara was preparing to go in for the kill, but they were interrupted by the Evans brothers.

"Isn't this sweet?" Chris Evans said sarcastically.

"Two girls fighting over the man they love," his twin brother Chuck agreed. Chris and Chuck were jocks, like Billy. They went everywhere together, and Lara thought it was creepy. If there was anyone at Cresswell that Lara hated more than Kim Marsh, it was the Evans boys.

"Give it a rest, gorillas," Lara told them, unafraid. Lara had heard that the Evans boys were real bullies, both on and off the playing field, but they had never given her a hard time before.

For once, Kim agreed with Lara. "Yeah, why don't you go pick on someone your own size?"

Chuck and Chris had a standard answer ready for this request. *"No* one is our size," they chanted in unison, then began striking body-builder poses in the middle of the hallway.

Lara was truly embarrassed by the scene she had caused. She and Kim stared at the Evanses, unimpressed, then got bored and walked off in different directions. From behind them, Chuck called, "You have been warned," and Chris added, "We'll be back," in a poor impression of the Terminator.

Lara couldn't find Billy all day, so she decided to stop by hockey practice after school to see if she could track him down there. She snuck into the rink at four o'clock, trying not to attract the attention—and ridicule—of the Evanses. She sat down in a corner of the stands.

Several rows in front of her, two middle-aged men in suits sat talking and taking notes on yellow pads of paper. Lara figured they must be college scouts who had come to check out Cresswell's star skater, Nick Glidden. She hoped they weren't impressed by the Evans boys. *Those Neanderthals don't deserve to go to college,* she thought.

The team of ten players stood at center ice, forming a circle around their coach, Len Murdock. Coach Murdock didn't know much about hockey strategy, but his wrestling squads were often among the best in the state. Budget cuts had forced coaches to double up on their team assignments, so Murdock took on hockey as well, even though he didn't know icing the puck from icing on a cupcake. Still, his players worshiped him.

Murdock had been around Cresswell forever. Both Billy's late father and Dr. Crandall had been state champion wrestlers for him back in '62. As a favor to her father, Coach Murdock had made it easy on Lara in sophomore gym class. She was a total klutz at athletics, but a bad grade in gym would have made a slight dent in her perfect grade-point average. Lara appreciated the slack he had cut her.

Billy was there, decked out in all his goalie's gear: mask, gloves, kneepads, and stick. He cut an imposing figure, but Lara's attention was focused on Nick Glidden. The fast-skating, high-scoring senior forward was tall and lean, with a mane of long blond hair that he tied up in a ponytail. Lara had the worst kind of crush on him.

She had thought about asking Billy to fix her up with Nick, but had never had the courage to pursue it. Nick never paid much attention to her. He was really popular—too popular. Lara thought she didn't really have a chance. Lara got asked out pretty often, but she had never been interested in having a steady boyfriend. There were boys at Cresswell whom she was friends with, like Billy and James, but Nick was the only one who really intrigued her, and he seemed unattainable.

The team went into a short scrimmage, and Lara watched intently as Nick beat Billy time after time for easy goals. Billy usually played pretty well in goal, but Nick was just too good for him. Lara felt sorry for Billy as he struggled to guard the net, but she got a secret, special thrill every time Nick scored.

After the practice broke up, the two men in suits charged over to Nick and started handing him brochures and patting him on the back. The Evans boys and a few others skated over and tried to ask the scouts questions about their programs, but the scouts were completely enthralled with Nick.

Billy finally spotted Lara in the stands and drifted over to her. "Hey, how long have you been sitting up there?" he asked, pulling his mask up over his curly reddish brown hair.

"Oh, just a little while. You looked great out there," she said, forcing a smile.

"Are you kidding? I got *murdered*. That's why those scouts are talking to Nick and not to me," Billy said with a tinge of bitterness.

Lara decided to change the subject. "You want to go grab a burger or something? There's something I've been meaning to ask you about."

Billy grinned. "It's a tempting offer, but I've got another practice. Coach Murdock is helping me and the Evanses get a head start on wrestling season with some private strength sessions." He looked down at the ice momentarily. "Gotta get pumped up for the spring season, when we go for the state title."

"You're going to run yourself ragged. How do you have any time left to study if you're practicing for two sports at once?" Lara asked with genuine concern.

Billy looked at her for a moment, then calmly said, "Homework is the least of my worries right now. There's no way my grades are going to get me into college, like you. A wrestling scholarship is the only chance I've got."

"Hey, Billy boy, you better go get ready for round two!" Coach Murdock called out from across the rink. "I've got some new drills for you boys that are going to knock your socks off."

"Look, we'll talk later, okay? Maybe this weekend we can get together," Billy said. He didn't wait for Lara's response before turning to skate to the locker room that connected the rink to the gymnasium.

Lara gathered up her books and started to leave, but saw Coach Murdock ambling clumsily across the ice toward her. "Hello there, young lady. Haven't seen you in a little while. How's your papa doing? It's been a while since he stopped by to see his old Coach."

"He's just fine—real busy down at the hospital. I'm sure he'll find time to come see at least one wrestling match this year. He always does," Lara said.

"Well, tell him I said hello," the Coach said.

Lara wanted to leave it at that—this was the longest conversation she'd ever had with Coach Murdock as it was—but there was one question she was dying to ask. "Coach Murdock, Billy told me about the extra wrestling practices he's been having. Are you sure that's a good idea? Don't you think he needs to use that time to try to bring up his grades?"

"Well, he asked me if I'd help him, and I wasn't about to say no. It's not often you see such drive in a young athlete," the Coach explained.

"Yes, but I'm worried that he's overdoing it. He's pinning all his hopes on getting a scholarship," Lara continued, but it was clear her words were falling on deaf ears.

Deep down, Lara wanted some reassurance that Billy would be all right after she left Cresswell for college. She had always worried about Billy. His mother hadn't been able to provide for him very well after she went back to work, but he'd been a good kid and stayed out of trouble—so far. His grades were barely passing, but Lara knew Billy wasn't stupid. He just had problems concentrating.

Lara wondered if Billy would have these problems if the accident had never happened. That was one of the things she wanted to talk to him about.

Coach Murdock assured Lara that Billy would be fine. "I know what's best for the boy. Don't you worry your pretty little head over him. Billy knows you can't survive in this world without a college degree, and I'm going to do everything in my power to see that he gets one."

For some reason she couldn't quite figure out, Coach Murdock's words rang hollow in Lara's ears. She left the rink more worried about Billy than ever.

Chapter 2

Lara rushed home from the rink. Her applications for college were coming due, and she hadn't yet completed the admission form for her top choice, Columbia University. She was angry at herself for putting it off until almost the last minute. This wasn't typical behavior for her; she'd never left an assignment to the last minute. So why was she procrastinating?

She knew why. She was terrified of being rejected. Lara had never failed at anything in her life. Her grades were always perfect, she always had plenty of friends, and she had even won the election for editor-in-chief of the school newspaper, over Betsy Gibson. Betsy had been the news editor junior year, the traditional stepping-stone to the top job, but Lara, a dark-horse candidate as features editor, had pulled off a major upset.

College was going to be different. She'd been a big fish in a small pond in Cresswell. But her application might not match up to the thousands of qualified students applying for admission to an Ivy League school like Columbia.

Of course, she had applied to other schools as well. Her guidance counselor, Mr. Crown, had seen to that. She had even applied to a small local college that she knew couldn't possibly reject her. "It's always good to have one school to fall back on in case of unforeseeable circumstances," Mr. Crown had told her.

The other applications had been easy. The essays she'd written so far had been strictly softball. She'd even used one of them twice, a one-pager on the historical figure whom she most admired. She figured everyone else would pick the obvious ones—George Washington, Abraham Lincoln, Martin Luther King. Lara only had to think for a minute to come up with her answer: Amelia Earhart, a strong woman who wasn't afraid to venture into the unknown.

Lara sat down at the dining-room table and faced up to her final application. She pulled out the thick envelope from her bookbag and took out the form. Rolling it into the electric typewriter on the table, she took a deep breath and began to peck away at the keys.

The top section was a snap; she'd typed her name, address, social security number, GPA, and class rank so many times now that she could have done it in her sleep. Some of the other information was a little more obscure, especially "educational history." Lara looked up the address of her elementary school again. And why did these colleges need to know her mother's maiden name? What good could that possibly do some college admissions officer?

The essay portion was the real challenge. It consisted of just one question, and they gave you two full pages to answer it, with a note saying you could attach white typing paper if you needed more room. The question was a tough one: What has been your most significant life experience?

Lara knew instantly what her answer would be, if she were completely honest: *the accident*. Nothing could compare in significance to that unforgettable event in Lara's life. But Lara wasn't about to make the mistake of being honest. Colleges wanted to read something positive, something upbeat. If Lara wrote about the accident that had taken her mother's (and Billy's father's) life, they might think she was some kind of depressed weirdo.

So what should it be? Lara sat puzzled for a few minutes. Then an idea came to her. She wanted to be a journalist, so her "significant life experience" should reflect that. She went to her bedroom and pulled her scrapbook off her bookshelf. Clippings of all the articles Lara had written for the school newspaper filled the pages. Surely she could find something of significance here.

No dice. As features editor, Lara had covered

school dances, Thespian Society drama productions, school band concerts . . . pretty innocuous stuff. After she'd been elected editor-in-chief, all she had written were the lead editorials. She didn't take a byline, since the views expressed were supposed to be those of the entire staff—and the paper hadn't tackled any issues tougher than a proposal for an extended lunch period, anyway. If she wrote about any of this stuff, Columbia would think she was an airhead.

There just weren't any hard issues facing the students at Cresswell. It wasn't Lara's fault, but she felt inadequate as a journalist as a result. Mrs. Alexander always told stories about how she had gotten started in journalism—covering the riots in her inner-city neighborhood during the civil rights movement of the sixties. Now, *that* was significant.

Lara had to face the facts: aside from the accident, she'd had a pretty easy life. Her life wasn't boring, but it certainly wasn't chock full of great events that lent themselves to this kind of essay. Frustrated, she dragged herself out of her room and plopped down on the living-room couch.

She picked up a copy of *Time* magazine that was lying on the coffee table, hoping to clear the cobwebs in her mind. Maybe reading an article about a current controversy would spur her thinking.

The cover story was on the savings-and-loan

crisis. Lara didn't even have her own checking account yet, so this didn't seem particularly relevant. The "World" section had an interesting article about racism in South Africa. Lara certainly had opinions about this issue—it seemed like a pretty clear-cut case of right and wrong—but the country seemed so far away.

Lara and her father hadn't traveled much since the trip to Canada. Going off to New York City for college seemed like an impossibly long journey to her. She had never even been there for a visit, though her father promised to take her there to look at Columbia if she got accepted.

Flipping past the movie reviews and the "People" section, Lara came to the "Health and Fitness" page, where an article caught her eye. According to a new study, up to ten percent of all male high-school athletes were taking anabolic steroids, synthetic male hormones designed to stimulate their muscle development artificially. Ninety-eight-pound weaklings were becoming musclemen practically overnight by taking these dangerous drugs.

Lara couldn't imagine anybody doing something so stupid, especially after she read about the side effects. Psychological damage—mood swings between depression and rage—affected many users immediately. Many experienced irrational, violent behavior. Long-term health risks included stunted growth and an increased chance of getting liver cancer.

As fascinating as the article was, Lara had to put it down and get back to work. *Time* magazine wasn't going to help her get into college. She couldn't waste any more time. She had to get back to her typewriter and come up with an answer.

Sitting there with a terminal case of writer's block, Lara couldn't keep herself from thinking about the steroids article. The picture of a smiling sixteen-year-old boy with grotesque muscles, sitting behind a table covered with the pills and needles that had made him so "strong," had burned itself into her mind.

Something clicked in Lara's head. One in ten high school athletes used these drugs. There were at least a hundred jocks at Cresswell. Could any of them be on steroids? It was an intriguing thought. If Lara could expose these drug abusers, her ability as an investigative reporter would be proven, and Columbia would never turn her down.

The next day at school, Lara stayed after journalism class to ask Mrs. Alexander how she should pursue this story. She waited until all the other kids had left the room. Lara knew this was going to be a big story, and she didn't want anyone—not even her staff—to know she was working on it.

As Mrs. Alexander listened patiently, Lara blurted out the information about steroids she'd learned from the article, and explained that she suspected this might be going on at Cresswell. Pausing to take a breath, Lara waited for Mrs. Alexander's congratulations on her initiative and insight as a reporter.

No congratulations were forthcoming. "Lara, you seem pretty worked up over this. Are you thinking rationally? A reporter needs to remain objective, and you seem to have come to a very strong conclusion based on very little—if any— real evidence," Mrs. Alexander told her.

Lara was crushed by Mrs. Alexander's lack of enthusiasm. "I know it sounds a little farfetched, Mrs. Alexander. But if I can get all the facts—the who, what, when, where, why, and how—we could have quite a story on our hands."

Mrs. Alexander put her arm around Lara. "Listen, I don't want to discourage you from looking into this story. I think it's great you're so fired up. But this is a very serious issue, and I don't want you to get ahead of yourself. You don't want to go around making accusations of criminal behavior based on a story you read in a magazine."

As always, Mrs. Alexander was right. Lara would have to proceed cautiously.

"So where do you suggest I begin?" she asked.

"Well, I don't think you should work alone on this project. That's not your job as editor-in-chief. You're supposed to delegate responsibility," Mrs. Alexander explained.

"But this is *my* story," Lara interrupted.

"No, Lara, you represent the whole paper. As editor, it's your job to know who can do this story best. I'm not saying you can't work on the story, and maybe even help write it *if* you come up with anything. But my job here is to train team players, not grandstanders."

"So who should I get to help?"

"You said this was a story about jocks. Who covers the jocks around here?" Mrs. Alexander asked.

Lara knew who Mrs. Alexander meant: James Horton. It made sense. As the sports editor, James knew all the players and the coaches. They trusted him, and so did Lara.

"Okay, so James and I will work together. Where do we start digging?"

"As I see it, there's no story yet—there's really just a hunch. A hunch can be important. All good reporters get them. To follow a hunch, you start talking to people. You know nothing. They may know something, but they're not going to tell you unless you ask," Mrs. Alexander said.

Lara realized now why she had talked to Mrs. Alexander. The woman was smart. Best of all, she knew how to speak directly to students without talking down to them. Lara thanked Mrs. Alexander, then rushed off to her next class. She was beginning to feel like a real reporter.

She ran into Ms. Wise's trigonometry class just as the bell rang. The class was a review for the next day's test. Lara had already finished preparing for it, so she pretended to take notes while making up a list of people she could talk to about steroids.

The first name came to her right away: Billy Owens. Lara could talk to him about anything—except the accident, that is. Maybe she wouldn't try to talk to him about the accident, after all. When they got together this weekend, Lara would say it was steroids she had wanted to discuss.

Lara remembered Mrs. Alexander's advice to stay calm and objective, but she didn't want to waste any time, either. She tracked Billy down in the hallway after lunch and asked him to come over for dinner Friday night. She knew her dad wouldn't mind. With the long hours that he had been working lately, he might not even be home.

"Sure, as long as you can make it kind of late," Billy said softly, glancing over his shoulder. "I've got wrestling practice with the Coach till seven."

Lara knew why he was acting so suspiciously. He wanted to make sure no one could overhear them and pass it along to Kim. Lara rolled her eyes, but she was excited to have lined up her first potential source for the story.

"By the way, what was it you wanted to talk to

me about so desperately the other day?" Billy asked.

Lara was caught off guard by his question. Should she lie? Say nothing and save it for Friday night? *Oh, what the heck,* she thought. *I'll go for it.*

"Steroids," she said simply.

To Lara's surprise, Billy's face turned chalky white. "Steroids?" he said, stammering slightly. "What about 'em?"

Lara saw how upset Billy was by the mere mention of the word. *What's wrong with him?* "Nothing," she said, eyeing him curiously. "I mean, I just read an article about them, and I was wondering what you know about them."

"What do I know about them? Nothing, that's what I know. Absolutely nothing." Billy looked as though he was about to faint.

"Billy, are you okay?" Lara asked.

Just then the Evans boys appeared out of nowhere. Chuck grabbed Billy from behind and put him in a full nelson. The jolt seemed to snap Billy out of his daze, and he began to laugh and struggle.

"Uncle!" he cried loudly, and Chuck let go. Chris was doubled over in hysterics.

Lara didn't find any of this funny. She just wanted to leave. "Forget about it, Billy. We can talk about it Friday night." As soon as she said that, she knew she was asking for grief from his subhuman friends.

Billy frowned as the Evanses began to hoot. "Loverboy's got a hot date!" Chris called at the top of his lungs. Chuck poked Billy from behind and made loud, disgusting kissing noises.

Lara had screwed this one up royally. Some sly reporter! All she'd succeeded in doing so far was scaring the wits out of Billy and humiliating both of them in front of half the school. She told Billy that she would see him Friday night, then walked away to the catcalls of Chuck and Chris.

Despite her embarrassment, Lara knew she had stumbled onto something big. She hadn't even considered the possibility that Billy himself might be taking steroids. She knew how hard he worked at his sports and had assumed his muscle development was the result of long hours in the weight room. But his shocked, defensive reaction to her question showed the possibility of another, more dangerous situation.

Chapter 3

"Gather 'round, champs! I've got a little surprise for you," Coach Murdock bellowed from the halfcourt of the gymnasium.

Billy, Chuck, and Chris came over from the corner mats where they were in the middle of a heated push-up contest. It was almost seven o'clock on Friday night, and all three were exhausted from their back-to-back hockey and wrestling practices.

The Coach immediately launched into one of his pep talks. "Now, I know you guys have been working hard this week, busting your behinds to be the best that you can be. I know you're tired, and you all want to go home and start your weekends. I even hear one of you has a hot date tonight." He nodded and grinned at Billy.

Billy turned bright red, his face flushed with anger and embarrassment. The Evans boys struggled to contain their laughter.

"QUIET!" the Coach screamed. "As I was saying, I know you're all bushed, but you know what?"

"WHAT?" his players barked in unison.

"I can't *hear* you!" the Coach yelled ferociously.

"WHAT?" they yelled at the top of their lungs.

Suddenly the Coach's voice dropped to an ominous whisper. Slowly he said, "I'm . . . not . . . quite . . . finished . . . with . . . you . . . yet." On the last word, he pulled a cord and a giant twine net fell from the rafters of the gym.

"I bought this off a fisherman friend of mine many years ago," Coach Murdock explained. "Climb to the top of it—using only your hands. When you make it to the top, touch the state championship pennant from 1962. Once you're back on the ground, you'll be dismissed for today. Any questions?"

"No, sir!" the boys responded as one.

"Then what are you waiting for? Start climbing!"

Billy took a running start and leaped onto the net. The twine cut into his hands, but he restrained himself from wincing. He remembered the Coach's motto: "Never let them see you hurt." Billy wouldn't allow anyone to have a psychological advantage over him, not an opponent, not a teammate, not even the Coach.

He climbed the net slowly, one hand over the other. He fought the temptation to take hold of the net with his feet, knowing that if he did, the

Coach would make him get down and climb it all over again. But each time he grabbed the net, his hands suffered new wounds. As he neared the top, he could feel a trickle of blood running down his arm.

Below him, the Coach was yelling encouragement, and the Evanses were goading him to climb faster so that they could have their turns. Billy didn't look down. He was almost thirty-five feet above the floor, and there were no mats below him. Billy was afraid of heights, but he was determined not to show his fear.

He continued to climb until he could reach the banner. Billy had looked up at that banner many times from the floor below, wishing that he could have seen his father wrestle for Coach Murdock's greatest team ever. He reached one shaking, blood-slick hand toward the banner and touched it. To the faint sound of cheers below, Billy quickly began his descent.

Coach Murdock slapped Billy on the back as Chuck jumped onto the net and began his struggle to the top. Billy didn't wait to see how Chuck and Chris did. He headed straight for the showers, knowing he was already late for dinner at Lara's house.

He tried to hurry, but he needed a long, hot shower to get rid of the grimy sweat. Then Billy paused for a moment and stood in front of the mirror, admiring his pumped-up physique. He was huge, his arms bulging with muscle. He looked great. Nothing could stop him now.

After taping up his bloodied hands, he pulled on his sweater and slammed his locker shut. The Evans twins burst through the gym door.

"Man, that was brutal!" Chris exclaimed, looking at his cut and bleeding hands.

"Intense!" his brother concluded.

"No pain, no gain," Billy reminded them as he tried to slip by them and out the door.

Chuck stood in his way. "Where do you think you're going?"

"You know where I'm going," Billy said, trying to step around Chuck's bulk.

"What's Kim got to say about this?" Chris wondered aloud.

"Kim doesn't have anything to do with this," Billy fired back. "Anyway, I'm going over to Lara's house for your sake as well as for mine."

"What?" the Evans boys said together.

"She asked me about steroids the other day," Billy said nervously. The twins' eyes almost popped out of their heads.

"What about them?" Chuck asked belligerently.

"Listen, I'm not sure what she knows. Maybe nothing. But I'm going to find out tonight. You guys stay out of it. She's my friend, and I can handle her," Billy told them.

"You're not going to tell her anything, are you?" Chris asked, his voice trembling slightly.

"Don't be an idiot. Of course not." Billy stepped around Chuck, who was standing straight and still, the look on his face as blank as a sheet of granite.

"I'll call you guys tomorrow and tell you what I found out." Billy walked out the door, leaving the Evans brothers staring silently at each other.

Lara was setting the table when her father walked in the front door at a quarter past seven. "Sorry I'm late, honey. The hospital was a nightmare, as usual." He put his medical bag down and looked through the day's mail.

"That's okay, Dad. Everybody's running a little late today. Billy's not here yet, and this lasagna is taking longer to cook than I expected," Lara said as she set her father's place at the head of the table.

"It smells delicious," Dr. Crandall told her. He walked over and kissed her on the forehead.

"Dad, can I talk to you about something?" Lara asked.

"Of course, honey. What is it? Is something wrong?" Her father took a seat at the table, ready to listen.

"I wasn't completely honest about why I invited Billy over for dinner," she began.

Her father perked up. "Are you two dating?"

"Dad! No!" Lara and her father were clearly not on the same wavelength. She would have to get right to the point.

"I think Billy may be involved with steroids," she said.

Her father looked at her in astonishment. "What makes you think that?" he asked.

"I read an article about steroid use in high school sports. Then when I brought up the topic with Billy, he acted really strange," Lara said.

"That doesn't make him guilty," Dr. Crandall said.

"I know that. But I want you to watch him this evening, observe his behavior. According to the article, steroids can affect your moods. And Billy's definitely been going through a lot of different moods lately," Lara continued.

"All adolescents are moody, Lara," her father said, adopting a tone of medical authority. "You certainly have your share of moods, but I'm not about to suggest that you're on steroids, or any other drugs for that matter."

Lara hated it when her father talked to her like she was one of his patients. "Dad, I don't have time to explain all this now. Just do me a favor and keep your mind open. Take a good look at Billy tonight. Look at how his muscles have grown all of a sudden. Then tell me if I'm crazy."

"This sounds like a normal teenager's development to me. Rapid changes in body and behavior are to be expected at this age. But, if it's important to you, I'll try to keep an eye out," Dr. Crandall reassured her.

"Thanks," Lara said.

The doorbell rang and the buzzer on the stove sounded simultaneously, causing Lara to jump slightly. "Could you get the door, Dad? I've got to get the lasagna." She hurried into the kitchen.

She heard her father greet Billy as she pulled the lasagna out of the oven. The cheese was bubbling, and Lara was careful not to burn herself on the pan. She put it down on the stove to cool and walked out into the living room. Billy and her father were looking through his old wrestling scrapbook.

"Hi, Billy. Dinner's almost ready," she said.

"Great. Your dad's just showing me some clippings from his championship season," Billy said without looking up from the book.

"We'll be there in a minute," her father said politely, giving Lara a quizzical look that she couldn't quite interpret. She went into the dining room, poured the drinks, and started to serve the salad.

Billy and her father sat down at the table as Lara was bringing in the main dish. "That looks terrific, Lara," Billy said. "Did you make that all by yourself?"

Lara smiled. "It's just a little something I whipped up after school."

"Oh, don't be so modest," her father teased her. "Lara's quite the little chef. I can barely make toast myself, but she's definitely inherited her mother's talents in the kitchen."

The mention of her mother made Lara feel uneasy all of a sudden. "So what happened to your hands? Did you hurt yourself?" Lara asked, looking down at Billy's bandaged mitts.

He defensively drew his hands under the table. "Sort of. It was a drill Coach Murdock had us do in practice today. Climbing a net. It was pretty hard, but I'm sure my hands will get used to it after a while."

"I can assure you that they will." Dr. Crandall laughed. "The Coach used to make us do that, too. Knowing him, it's probably the same net."

Lara was shocked by this barbaric exercise, but she tried not to show it. After she served the lasagna to Billy and her father, she took a good look at Billy, trying to see him objectively. She realized with surprise that the skinny kid she had grown up with had developed into a thickly muscled teenager. His arms were enormous, and veins stood out beneath the skin. His chest, under the sweater, was as big as a barrel. Even his neck seemed corded with muscle.

But to Lara's dismay, Billy was showing no signs of mood swings. He seemed perfectly content to sit and shoot the breeze with her father about wrestling for Cresswell. Her father would be even less willing to believe that Billy was involved with steroids after this. *But how can he ignore how big Billy is?* Lara thought angrily.

Lara excused herself from the table for a moment when Billy and her father were helping themselves to seconds. She went to the bathroom, splashed a little cold water on her face, then paused for a moment in the living room to gather her thoughts before returning to the table. *Now what?* She would have to get Billy alone.

Suddenly something caught her eye. Billy's gym bag was sitting on the couch next to the scrapbook. Lara was seized with curiosity and ambition. She knew if she could find physical evidence of steroids in Billy's gym bag, she'd have her first real lead in the story. She also knew how wrong it would be to look through his bag, and that it would be evidence that was illegally obtained.

She went ahead and did it anyway. As she listened intently to make sure her father and Billy were still wrapped up in conversation, she slowly pulled open the drawstrings and reached inside.

Holding her breath, she fumbled through his sweaty gym clothes and bundled-up socks, and found an unused syringe. Lara stared at the needle, her heart pounding, excited by the discovery but horrified by the implications. Just then conversation came to a lull in the dining room. Lara stuffed the needle back in the bag, pulled the drawstrings tight, and hopped up from the couch.

She walked into the dining room and sat down, quickly regaining her composure. "You guys must have really liked dinner. There's hardly any food left," she said, trying to sound cheery.

As her father and Billy complimented her cooking, Lara's mind was filled with thoughts. Did Billy use the needle to take steroids? What other explanation could there be? He wasn't a diabetic, as far as Lara knew. What other kind of shots did people give themselves? She tried to stay focused on the conversation through dessert, but it wasn't easy. Luckily, Billy and her father had plenty to say to each other.

By nine o'clock, Billy and Dr. Crandall were all talked out, and Lara offered to walk Billy outside. Dr. Crandall said good-bye to him warmly and closed the door behind them.

Billy sat down on the swing on the front porch and motioned for Lara to join him. She was in no mood to chat, but she couldn't let Billy know how flustered she was.

Looking up at the moon, Billy asked her, "Now, what was this you wanted to talk about the other day—drugs or something?"

This was the last topic Lara wanted to talk about right now. She needed some time to figure out her next move. "Oh, it was nothing, Billy," she bluffed.

Billy looked down at Lara. "It didn't seem like it was nothing the other day."

"It was just some silly article I read in a magazine about steroids. I didn't know much about them, so I wanted to find out more. I figured with you being an athlete, you might know a little more. But obviously you don't," Lara said innocently.

"No, I don't know anything about them, except that they're supposed to be dangerous," Billy said ominously. "The less you know about them, the better off you'll be."

Lara carefully schooled her face to show no expression. But surely Billy was warning her.

"Like I said," she repeated, "it was nothing."

Billy couldn't quite leave it at that. "And that's all you know about steroids . . . what you read in that article?"

Lara noticed the sound of relief in Billy's voice. "Not a thing more," she told him.

Billy thanked Lara again for dinner and started to walk home. Lara watched him until he was almost out of sight, then turned and walked back into the house.

Lara knew now that she hadn't dreamed up this story. The needle, Billy's veiled warning to avoid the subject . . . it all seemed to be adding up. On Mrs. Alexander's advice, she planned to proceed with caution. She would ask James to help her first thing Monday morning, and together they would get to the bottom of the story before writing a single word. They would approach the assignment responsibly. Lara didn't want to destroy Billy's reputation. She told herself that by exposing steroid usage at Cresswell, she could save him from even greater danger.

Chapter 4

Billy had known that it would be a long walk home from Lara's house, at least three miles. He had walked there after practice, which was a little more than a mile, but his house was two miles in the opposite direction from the school. Still, Billy had felt as if he had little choice. His bike was broken and he couldn't afford to get it fixed, since he needed to save up to take Kim to the winter semiformal dance next month. His mother had taken the family car, a beat-up old station wagon, to work. Billy hated it when his mom's boss scheduled her for the late shift at the diner on Friday night. It put a serious crimp in his social life—no wheels on the biggest date night of the week.

He could have asked Lara to drive him home —after all, she had her own little blue Honda Civic. But he couldn't swallow his pride to ask her for a ride. Besides, he didn't want to let Lara see what a dump he lived in.

As close as they had remained over the years, Lara had never been to Billy's house since he moved out of Gaspee Farms. He guessed that Lara was afraid to venture into his dangerous neighborhood, and he hadn't encouraged her. Billy was ashamed of his house; although he kept the lawn in great condition, the house itself looked very run-down, even by the standards of the Lower Basin. The paint on the outside was peeling badly, and two of the shutters were missing.

"This will be good aerobic exercise," Billy told himself as he walked alone in the dark, passing by the beautiful houses of his old neighborhood. He thought about trying to jog home, but his gym bag was weighing him down. It was stuffed full with his usual gear, plus a few textbooks he had brought home in the unlikely event he would have some time to study over the week-end.

He felt much better after talking to Lara. He had been paranoid that somebody might find out his secret, but he knew nobody would squeal. No one "in the know" about the steroids would have anything to gain by talking to Lara or anybody else about it.

Billy reached into his bag to make sure that his needle was still there. He found the syringe and breathed a sigh of relief. He had gotten in the habit of constantly checking to make sure his pills and needles were with him at all times. A few weeks ago, Billy had accidentally left an unused syringe in his gym locker and had to go running back to the school at midnight to retrieve it. You couldn't leave evidence like that lying around.

He walked by the school and looked up at the lettering on the side of the building: CRESSWELL HIGH SCHOOL. Mini-searchlights shined up on the letters, casting long, weird shadows on the red brick wall.

Billy walked up to the door of the gym and looked inside. The lights were off, and the net he had struggled to climb earlier that day was hanging undisturbed up in the rafters. Billy's eyes were drawn to the championship banner next to it. Was he really able to climb high enough to touch it? It seemed like a dream, like he could fly.

He fumbled around in his pocket for the gym key that Coach Murdock had given him and a few other trusted players in case they wanted to come in and practice after hours. He found it and unlocked the door, still staring up at the banner, transfixed.

Walking inside, Billy decided not to switch on the lights. Smitty, the cranky old janitor who watched the school building at night, might be sleeping under the bleachers again, and Billy knew it was best not to wake him. Billy's sneakers squeaked softly on the gym floor as he walked toward midcourt.

He couldn't take his eyes off the banner. He felt dizzy just thinking about how high he had climbed. Sure, he had been scared once he was actually up there, but a psychologist he had seen on TV had said that the way to conquer a fear is to confront it. Billy had done just that by climbing to the ceiling of the gym.

Yet something about Billy's triumph seemed incomplete and artificial. He knew what had given him the strength to climb so high: hard work, determination, the support of Coach Murdock . . . and drugs. Could he have achieved the kind of strength it took to climb that net without taking the steroids?

He looked up at the banner again, and at the net perched next to it. Billy knew his father had been a state championship wrestler—without taking steroids. They didn't even exist back in 1962. Would his father have taken steroids if they had been available? Billy tried to convince himself that his father would have wanted to win at all costs, but inside he knew that this wasn't true.

He felt a drop of liquid on his face and brushed it away with his hand. Was the roof leaking again? He looked up at the ceiling and saw the net dripping blood on him. His heart skipped a beat and he took off running toward the bright red Exit sign. His shoulder smashed into the door, but he didn't stop running even after he heard it crash closed behind him.

He ran full speed across the parking lot and looked back only when he got to the other side of the street. He brushed another drop from his face. It was a tear. Had the net really been dripping blood? Was he hallucinating? Billy was too scared to go back and check it out.

He started walking home again, shakily whistling the school fight song as he made his way down the dark streets of Cresswell. Cars whizzed by him on either side as he reached the main strip of the Lower Basin.

The liquor stores and fast-food restaurants were closing up now. It was almost ten o'clock. Billy turned off the main street and started walking down the hill that led to his house. Suddenly a car screamed off the road and cut in front of him, swerving into the driveway he was just about to walk across. Billy jumped instinctively back out of the car's path, and his gym bag went flying across the pavement.

The car came to a screeching stop and the doors flew open. As Billy frantically retrieved his bag, two hulking figures wearing ski masks charged out of the car and tackled him. One of them pounded Billy's head against the sidewalk as the other tied his arms behind his back and bound him at the ankles. Billy's head was reeling with pain, and he couldn't put up much of a struggle. The two attackers lifted Billy and threw him in the back seat of their car. They slammed the doors behind them and sped off down the hill.

It all happened so fast. Billy didn't know what

had hit him. He rolled off the back seat and landed with a thud on the floor. He wasn't gagged, but he was swimming in too much pain and confusion to call for help. The car went screaming around corners as Billy floated in and out of consciousness. In his more clear-thinking moments, he hoped a cop would pull the car over for the way these maniacs were driving. Then he could get their attention. He tried to concentrate, to think about who these guys were and where they were taking him.

Were these just random hoodlums, or was someone trying to get revenge on Billy? But for what? He couldn't think of anyone who had a serious grudge against him. All he could see from the floor of the back seat was cheap automobile carpet, which the blood from his head wound was slowly staining red. Billy closed his eyes and tried to keep himself from passing out again.

The car slowed down, and Billy heard the driver switch off the headlights. The two men hadn't spoken a word to each other for the whole ride, but then one of them said, "Is this the place?" and Billy immediately recognized the slight lisp in the voice. It was Chris Evans!

"Yeah," the driver answered, and Billy knew that it must be Chuck behind the wheel. It figured that Chuck would be the one in the driver's seat—he was always bullying his less intelligent twin.

Billy's mind raced with questions. What had he done to the Evans boys to deserve this? What were they going to do with him? Where were they going? Should he let on that he knew it was them? Nothing made sense to Billy, so he pretended to be unconscious until the car stopped.

The brothers jumped out, then pulled Billy out of the back seat and started dragging him along the ground. Billy opened one eye and saw that they were at Pine Lake, five miles outside Cresswell. The brothers had parked their car next to the shore and were hauling Billy's limp body toward the water.

As far as Billy could tell, they had every intention of throwing his body into the water and leaving him to drown. This was clearly no prank, and if Billy didn't do something fast, he was going to be dead in a matter of minutes. He yelled out "Help!" at the top of his lungs, and the startled boys dropped his legs like hot potatoes.

"He's awake!" Chris cried.

"Hit him again!" Chuck screamed.

Billy wriggled on the ground and yelled, "Chuck and Chris Evans are trying to kill me!" All he heard in response was a faint echo in the distance.

"Shut up!" Chuck said angrily. "We're not going to kill you."

"What do you call this?" Billy asked desperately. "A surprise party?"

"What are we supposed to do?" Chuck

snarled back at him. "Sit back and let you turn us all in to Lara Crandall as steroid users?"

"Are you insane? What makes you think I would tell Lara anything?" Billy said, lying on the grassy shore.

Chuck shook his head violently in disbelief. "We drove by and saw you sitting on Lara's porch tonight. What else would you two talk about? You told us she knew about the steroids. What did you tell her?"

"Nothing," Billy said, feeling faint again. His hands were numb below the tight ropes.

"WHAT?" Chuck bent down and screamed in Billy's face.

"NOTHING!" Billy yelled back at him.

"Hey, man, maybe he's telling the truth," Chris said to his seething brother.

Chuck turned around and pushed his brother to the ground. "Shut up! We have to look out for ourselves!"

"It was just a thought," Chris said under his breath as he got up, brushed off his jeans, and pulled off his ski mask.

"What are you doing?" Chuck charged at him again.

Chris ducked out of the way, and Chuck tripped and fell onto the ground next to Billy. "Billy knows that it's us, Chuck. What difference does it make if we keep our masks on?"

Chuck buried his head in his hands. "Okay, you're in charge!"

Billy managed to sit up, and he looked straight at Chris. "Don't let him push you around, man. I'm not going to rat on you guys, not for using steroids, not even for beating me up. You're my friends."

Chuck punched Billy hard in the side of the head, reopening the wound from the sidewalk pounding. Glaring at Chris, he jumped to his feet, ran back to the car, and took a long piece of rope out of the trunk. He tied it to Billy's ankles and threw one end over the limb of a tree that stretched out over the river.

"We'll see if he's telling the truth," Chuck said as he began to pull on the end of the rope, lifting Billy up off the ground by his feet.

Chris stood silently as Chuck pulled with all his might to raise Billy's feet up to the edge of the limb, suspending him upside down fifteen feet above the water.

Billy felt the blood rushing to his head and dripping down into the water. The world was spinning furiously, and he could barely hear Chuck yelling accusations from the edge of the water: "You were going to turn us in, weren't you? *Weren't you?*"

Chris's voice pleaded in the background to let Billy go, but Chuck shouted him down. "Admit it!" Chuck screamed at Billy. "Admit you're a traitor!"

It was too much for Billy—the throbbing pain, the rushing blood, the dizzying height, the insistent accusations. He had to say something to make it all go away. He was ready to make a false confession when the rope at his ankles snapped from his weight.

Billy felt himself falling rapidly toward the water. It seemed forever before he hit the surface, but then the cold water slapped him across the face and everything went dark.

As his body sank like a rock to the bottom of the lake, Billy struggled to untie the rope around his wrists, but it was no use. The tears from his eyes mixed with the lake water that was slowly filling his lungs.

Chapter 5

Lara had trouble falling asleep after Billy left her house. She was all wound up over the prospect of launching her first real investigative report. After re-reading the *Time* article and watching a news report on recruiting violations in college basketball, Lara got in bed at eleven and tried to make herself fall asleep.

She had to get up early in the morning and go down to the public library to look for more articles on steroids. But sleep didn't come easily. She tossed and turned for a couple of hours, then went downstairs for a glass of milk. Wandering into her father's study, she decided to look through his medical books to see if she could find information about steroids. She took a thick volume on prescription drugs from the shelf and started flipping the pages.

Just as she got to the section on steroids, Lara heard her father coming downstairs and slammed the book shut. Her father peeked in the door to the study and asked, "Is everything okay, honey?"

"Fine, Dad. I'm sorry if I woke you up."

"Don't worry about it," her father said, rubbing the sleep out of his eyes. "What'cha reading?"

"Nothing," Lara said, putting the book back on the shelf. "These boring medical books usually put me right to sleep, but I guess it's not going to work tonight."

Her father smiled sympathetically. "Insomnia can be murder. I think you'll have a better chance of falling asleep if you lie in bed and rest your eyes," he said.

"Thanks, Dad. Good night," Lara said, rushing upstairs.

"G'night," her father mumbled as he followed her.

Lara lay in bed, staring straight up at the ceiling for a few minutes. Then she began to feel her eyelids getting heavy. Soon she was fast asleep, and the nightmares began again.

It was the same horrible dream that she had had so many times over the years: her mother getting farther away from her, the twisted metal hurtling toward the car window, the blood gushing out of her mother's neck—until she turned around to look at Billy in the back seat. Instead of the frightened eight-year-old boy reaching out one blood-soaked hand toward her, Lara saw Billy as he had appeared at dinner that night, a strapping young athlete with heavy white bandages on his hands.

His father was no longer sitting next to him, but his mother lay slumped at his side. Billy smiled at Lara, but then she noticed that the bandages on his hands were turning red. Billy screamed out in pain, but Lara didn't know how to help him.

She grabbed his gym bag from the seat beside him and searched through it for more bandages. The bag was filled with hundreds of syringes. Billy's screams grew louder and more tortured, until Lara grabbed one of the needles and drove it into his heart, silencing him forever.

The phone rang loudly in Lara's ear, and she leaped out of bed. Glancing at her clock, she saw that it was six-thirty in the morning. Her heart in her throat, she managed to whisper, "Hello?" into the receiver.

The voice on the other end sounded very far away. "Lara, it's Rita Owens. I'm sorry to wake you. Is your father home?"

Lara couldn't quite put everything together for a minute. She was still stuck in the dream, where Mrs. Owens was lying passed out on the back seat. "Is something wrong?" Lara asked, trying to shake some sense back into her head.

Mrs. Owens's voice began to break. "Billy didn't come home last night. He told me he was eating dinner at your house. Did he spend the night there?"

The panic in Mrs. Owens voice brought Lara back to earth. "No, he left here around nine."

There was a long silence, and Lara tried to think of something reassuring to say. She stammered, "I—I'm sure he's fine. You know guys . . ."

Mrs. Owens regained her composure. "I know you're probably right, Lara, but I'm worried about Billy. I'm going to call the police. Thank you, and I'm sorry to disturb you this early in the morning."

Before Mrs. Owens could hang up, Lara asked, "Is there anything we can do to help?"

Again there was a long silence, then Mrs. Owens said, "I'll let you know," and hung up the phone.

Lara didn't know what to think. She got out of bed and went to wake up her father. "Billy's disappeared!" she announced, and he sat up, startled.

"Huh?"

"That was Mrs. Owens on the phone, Dad. Billy didn't come home last night."

Dr. Crandall reached over to the nightstand and put on his glasses. Running his fingers through his sleep-tossed hair, he said, "Well, I'm sure he's fine. Wrestlers can get pretty rowdy. He and his friends probably stayed out all night partying." He smiled and looked up at the ceiling. "I remember some pretty crazy shindigs we threw before going into training. . . ."

"Dad, this is serious!" Lara said.

Dr. Crandall frowned. "Go back to bed, Lara.

Frankly, I'm much more concerned about you than I am about Billy. You've been acting very strangely lately. The nightmares, the insomnia —these could be warning signs of something serious."

This was too much for Lara. She marched out of the room and started downstairs. "*You* can go back to bed, Dad. I'm going down to the police station."

Dr. Crandall came after her. "You're going nowhere, young lady!" he said, grabbing her arm.

Lara pulled away. "I have my own car. I can go wherever I want!"

She ran downstairs, and Dr. Crandall tried to regain his composure. "Fine, Lara, you go to the police station. What good is it going to do you?"

"I'll report Billy as a missing person. Then the police will start looking for him," she said angrily.

"Billy hasn't even been 'missing' for twelve hours yet. Someone's got to be gone for forty-eight hours before the police will even consider beginning a search," Dr. Crandall said, lapsing into the know-it-all tone that drove Lara crazy.

Lara didn't understand her father. Wasn't he the least bit concerned about Billy? Didn't he realize that Billy wasn't like the party-animal jocks who ran around until all hours of the morning? Lara knew that Billy was in real trouble.

She threw on some clothes and looked around

for her car keys. Dr. Crandall gave up and retreated to his room in disgust. Lara left the
house and got into her car. She simply couldn't
wait any longer. Her investigation into Billy
Owens's disappearance and its relationship to
possible steroid use at Cresswell High would
have to begin right now.

Chapter 6

Lara pulled up to the police station and parked next to the paddy wagon. It was just past seven, so there wasn't much activity around the station house. Cresswell had its share of crimes, but this early on Saturday morning almost everyone in town, including the criminals, was still in bed. Lara walked quickly into the building and approached a potbellied officer reading the morning newspaper behind the front counter.

The policeman didn't seem to notice Lara. He dipped a glazed doughnut into his mug of coffee and continued reading the sports section.

Lara finally spoke up. "Excuse me, officer?"

A grizzled voice came from behind the newspaper. "Yeah?"

"I'd like to report a missing person," she said calmly.

The policeman remained silent for a moment, then leaned forward in his chair, folded his newspaper neatly on his desk, and took a sip of coffee. He grimaced as he swallowed the hot black liquid, then asked, "How long's he been missing?" Lara had been hoping this question wouldn't come up, but she had to answer it honestly. "Almost twelve hours."

The officer shot her an incredulous look, and Lara looked down at the counter in embarrassment. She stared blankly at the officer's tarnished nameplate. It read: "Ofcr. Roy Hendrikson."

Hendrikson cleared his throat and said, "I'm afraid you're gonna need to wait a couple of days. If the person doesn't turn up by Monday, come back and file a report."

"You don't understand. I can't wait," Lara pleaded.

"Why?" Hendrikson asked, his brow furrowed. "Is it one of your parents? Well, you should have said so. In that case, we can start looking right away. State law says that minors can't be left unsupervised for any prolonged period of time."

"I'm not a minor, and it's not one of my parents. It's a friend of mine. Billy Owens," Lara explained.

"How old is your friend?"

"He's seventeen."

"Is he your boyfriend?"

Lara didn't think this was any of Officer Hendrikson's business. She fidgeted and didn't answer his question.

Hendrikson got up out of his seat and started walking Lara to the door. "Look, sounds to me

like your friend Billy stayed out all night partying. We have no evidence to indicate other-
wise. . . ."

Lara wasn't about to give up. "But he's been
having a lot of problems lately," she said.

Hendrikson paused for a moment. "What
kind of problems? Is he into drugs?"

Lara didn't know how to answer that. Billy
was into drugs, but not the kind the officer was
talking about. She didn't have enough evidence
to tell him about the steroids. She just wanted
them to start looking for Billy.

"He's been having personal problems," she
said, not elaborating.

"Trouble at home?" the officer asked.

"Sort of." Lara shrugged.

"So you think maybe he ran away from
home?" Hendrikson asked.

Lara could tell she was going to get nothing
accomplished here. "No, he wouldn't do that."

Hendrikson shook his head and began escort-
ing Lara toward the door again. "Oh, you'd be
surprised how many kids run away because of
personal problems. But, as I said, we can't start
looking for him for another thirty-six hours."

"That may be too late!" Lara said desperately.

Hendrikson held the door open for Lara. "Unless the kid has committed some kind of crime,
or we have evidence that he's become the vic-
tim of foul play, there's nothing else we can do.

I'm sorry. I know you're upset, but that's just the way it is."

Lara thanked the officer—*for nothing*, she thought—and walked to her car. She sat there for a moment, not knowing where to go. She was still too mad at her father to go home. He would be waiting to say "I told you so." Lara didn't want to give him the satisfaction.

The library wouldn't open for another two hours. Cruising the streets of Cresswell looking for Billy was definitely out. The most likely spots to find him were in the Lower Basin, and Lara was afraid to go there by herself, even during the day.

She decided to drive over to James Horton's house and ask him to help her in the investigation. Lara remembered where his house was in Gaspee Farms from last year's Halloween party. His parents were vacationing in Europe, so she knew she didn't have to worry about waking them. Of course, James would probably still be in bed at this hour, but once Lara filled him in on the details of her investigation, he would probably thank Lara for opening his eyes to it. As an aspiring sportswriter, he would definitely be interested in this story.

Lara pulled into the Hortons' driveway and shut off the engine. She walked up to the door and knocked softly. There was no answer. She knocked louder and finally heard movement inside.

"Coming!" James called out groggily. "Who is it?"

"It's Lara."

"Who?" The door opened, and James stood before Lara in a tattered blue bathrobe and pajama bottoms. Startled to see her, he clutched his bathrobe closed. "Lara! What are you doing here?"

"Sorry to wake you." Lara blushed.

James fumbled to fix his tousled hair. "What's up?"

"It's a long story," Lara said wearily. "Can I come in?"

James took a step back and invited her into the living room. "Yeah, sure."

"Thanks," Lara said, taking a seat on the couch.

"You want some juice or something? Or you want to join me in some Crunchberries?" James offered.

Lara laughed. It was the first time she had laughed since she had stumbled onto the steroids story. She felt guilty enjoying herself, especially when she thought Billy was in trouble. But James was a genuinely funny guy, even at seven-thirty in the morning.

"No, thanks. But you better pour yourself a big bowl," Lara said. "I've got quite a story to tell you."

* * *

James sat silently, occasionally spooning a bite of cereal into his mouth, as Lara recounted everything she knew about the steroids story so far. After she finished describing her useless visit to the police station, she said, "Then I came here. I need your help. So what do you say?"

"What do I say? I say this sounds like a major, major story. We're talking Pulitzer Prizes here."

Lara was glad that James was as excited about the story as she was. Finally, someone saw how significant this investigation could be. "So what do you think we should do next?" she asked.

"Let's put the story to the Sarah Jane Alexander test to see how much of it you've got so far. I'll ask the questions, and you give me the answers, okay?"

Lara nodded, and James began the familiar litany of questions. "Who?"

"Billy, the Evanses, maybe more athletes to be named later."

"Good. What?"

"Use of steroids to artificially enhance muscle development."

"Right. When?"

Lara thought for a second. "That one's hard to pin down exactly. The article that I read said that steroids are usually taken over a six- to twelve-week period. The pills come first, followed by injections. Billy's still taking injections, and they've clearly started to show their effects.

So my educated guess is that they have been taking the steroids for about two months."

"Excellent deduction," James congratulated her. "Where?"

"Cresswell High School. Athletic Department."

"Why?"

"I know that Billy is determined to get a wrestling scholarship to college. The Evans boys certainly aren't going to get into college based on their SAT scores either. They're taking the steroids to give themselves an advantage in wrestling. If they can win the state, they can get into college with scholarships."

"Flawless reasoning. Okay, last question. How?"

She couldn't come up with an answer. In fact, she wasn't even sure what the question meant in this case.

"How what?" she asked James.

"We already did 'what'—steroids," James corrected her.

"No, I mean, what question beginning with 'how' do we need to answer in order to have a complete story?"

James scratched his head. "Gee, that's a good question. Wait, I got it—how did they get the steroids in the first place? There's got to be a supplier, a connection somewhere. We're talking about Mr. Big here."

Lara didn't have any idea where they had

gotten the steroids. She hadn't even thought about this part of the investigation yet. "I'm clueless on this," she admitted.

"That's cool," James consoled her. "Now we know what we need to find out next to get the final piece of the puzzle—the identity of the supplier."

Lara could see that James was getting carried away with the story—as carried away as she had been when she first found out about it.

"Slow down, Speedy Gonzalez," she told him. "We're not anywhere near the end of the story. We're still working on hunches and circumstantial evidence. Finding a needle in Billy's gym bag—during a highly unethical and probably illegal search of it—is not enough evidence to win us a Pulitzer Prize."

James knew Lara was right. "Listen to you . . . you sound like Mrs. Alexander."

"I'll take that as a compliment. She's a very smart woman. After all, who do you think suggested that I get you to help me on this story?"

James chuckled. Lara got back to business. "So how do we go about finding the supplier?"

"You're the expert on steroids. How do other kids get them? Are they illegal? Do they buy them on a street corner or from the drugstore or what?" James quizzed her.

"I don't think they're strictly illegal," Lara began, "but they are banned from all forms of athletics. I guess they're like prescription drugs that you can get from a pharmacy with a physician's signature."

"Okay, then I'll investigate the local pharmacies. I've got some friends who work at drugstores. Maybe they've seen Billy or the Evanses come in to pick up their dope."

"Good idea. And I'll do some more research to find out if there are other ways to get steroids," Lara volunteered.

"Great." James got up to take his cereal bowl into the kitchen. He stopped in the doorway and turned to Lara. "Hey, you don't think Coach Murdock could be Mr. Big, do you?"

Lara tried to keep in mind Mrs. Alexander's advice not to make accusations against people without evidence. But discussing a hunch with a fellow reporter on the case didn't seem wrong.

"He would seem to be the most likely suspect," she said. "Of course, this is just intuition, but he was acting pretty weird when I talked to him the other day. He's got this win-at-any-cost attitude. I wonder if that includes getting his kids hooked on dangerous drugs."

"I've never liked the guy, to tell you the truth," James said. "He always seemed like one of those cult leaders who brainwashes his followers."

"We're getting into some pretty heavy-duty character assassination here," Lara warned him. "Let's take a step back for a second. We've got nothing on this guy."

"Not yet," James insisted. "But maybe we should set up an interview with him on Monday. We could pull a *60 Minutes* on him—grill him about steroids and try to get him to admit that he's involved."

"Talking to Coach Murdock isn't a bad idea," Lara mused. "My dad's got his home number. I'll give him a friendly call today and ask if you and I can interview him on Monday about wrestling. Then, when we get him alone in his office with a tape recorder, we'll give him the third degree."

"Great plan," James agreed.

Lara left James's house excited about their strategy to crack the steroids case. She wondered if it was wrong to enjoy the investigation so much. These were serious matters that she was dealing with—and Billy was still missing, after all. As anxious as Lara was to find out the truth, she was scared that it might be worse than her most awful nightmares.

Chapter 7

Lara avoided talking to her father as much as possible for the rest of the weekend. She spent most of the day Saturday in the library reading articles about steroids. At dinnertime she came home and fixed herself a sandwich, not asking her father if he wanted one. Then she shut herself in her room and read for the rest of the evening.

Lara wanted her father to know she was upset. She had gotten her stubbornness from him, and neither one was about to apologize. Lara wanted her father to treat her like an adult and respect her investigation. She was tired of being treated like a little girl who didn't know what was going on in the world around her.

On Sunday morning, Lara got up early and sneaked downstairs. Searching through her father's briefcase, she found Coach Murdock's telephone number in his address book. She jotted it down on a scrap of paper and dropped the book back into the briefcase when she heard her father coming downstairs.

Lara bolted to the front door and brought in the Sunday paper. She glared at her father as they passed on his way to the kitchen. Sitting down on the couch, she pulled out the funnies and began to laugh at "Calvin and Hobbes," her favorite strip.

Dr. Crandall wandered into the living room with his English muffin and coffee and sat next to Lara on the couch. She ignored him. He was clearly trying to make peace, but Lara would have nothing of it.

"Can you pass me the front section?" he asked his daughter in a very polite tone.

Lara handed him the front page. Dr. Crandall took it, and the two sat silently on the couch for a few moments reading to themselves.

"The Far Side" made Lara burst out laughing again. "What's so funny?" her father asked, peering over her shoulder.

Lara said nothing, but held the cartoon in front of her father to read. He looked at it for a minute and said, "I don't get it."

"Humor isn't funny if you have to explain it," Lara mumbled.

Her father shrugged and started reading again. "Says here that Gorbachev may be stopping in Cresswell during his next visit to the States," he told Lara. "He wants to see a typical American town."

"Yeah, I heard about it on the radio last night.

Gorbymania hits Cresswell. Big whoop," Lara said derisively.

Dr. Crandall broke the ice. "Look, honey, I understand that you're worried about Billy. I am, too. But there's nothing we can do about it right now, so it doesn't make any sense for you to be mad at me."

Lara had been waiting for her father to say something like this. Now she could tell him what she really thought. "There *is* something that I can do to help Billy, and I'm doing it. I think he's mixed up in steroids. The steroids have something to do with his disappearance, and I'm going to get to the bottom of it. But you're not supporting me. You're treating me like a little kid!"

"I just don't want you to get in over your head," Dr. Crandall explained. "You're on a wild-goose chase with this steroids thing. You got the idea planted in your head and you can't get it out. I see it happen with my patients all the time. It's called 'hypochondria': a patient reads about a disease and convinces himself that he has it. In this case, you read about steroids and convinced yourself that Billy was taking them."

Lara was fed up with her father's diagnoses of her problems. "I know what hypochondria is, and I'm not a hypochondriac. I don't even see what this has to do with anything."

"Lara, I support you in *everything* you do. I

always have. I'm just trying to save you from getting hurt. It's a mistake for you to pursue this story any further. If Billy doesn't come home by tomorrow, the police will look for him. Leave it up to them. They're the experts."

Lara simmered silently. She could see her father wasn't going to be convinced. *That's okay,* she told herself. She could do it without his help.

"Think about what I said, Lara," Dr. Crandall said, getting up off the couch. "I've got a golf date this morning. We can talk about this more tonight."

"Whatever," Lara said.

Lara impatiently folded and refolded the piece of paper with Coach Murdock's phone number on it as she listened to her father taking a shower. Finally, he emerged from his room in a garish green plaid outfit, carrying his clubs.

"No hard feelings?" he asked as he walked to the front door.

"No hard feelings," she answered in a humble tone. She would have said anything to make him leave.

As soon as she heard her father's car pull out of the driveway, Lara dialed Coach Murdock's number.

The Coach answered on the first ring. "Hello?"

"Coach Murdock?" Lara asked in her sweetest voice, "This is Lara Crandall. I'm sorry to disturb you at home. I hope I didn't wake you."

"That's all right. Actually, I was on my way out the door. What can I do for you this fine morning?"

"The school paper is planning on doing a big story on the wrestling team. Everyone says we may win the state this year," she said.

"I think we've got the best bunch of boys since your daddy's squad," the Coach agreed.

"Our sports editor, James Horton, and I would like to interview you tomorrow afternoon about the wrestling team. Would that be okay?"

"Why, sure. I'd be happy to grant you an audience. Be in my office at three o'clock sharp," the Coach said.

"Yes, sir," Lara said enthusiastically. "Thank you, sir."

"See you tomorrow, then. Good-bye."

Lara hung up the phone. The trap was set. Tomorrow it would be sprung. She called James to tell him the good news.

Dr. Crandall came home from the country club late that afternoon. Lara was up in her room preparing questions for her interview with Coach Murdock.

"Honey?" her father called from the bottom of the stairs. "Can you come down here a minute?"

Lara walked to the top of the stairs. "What is it?"

"Do you know who I played golf with today?"

"No. Should I?"

"Coach Murdock. I called him up and asked him to play after talking to Billy the other night," he said.

Lara's heart fell into her stomach. Had her father told the Coach about her steroids investigation? This could be disastrous!

"He said you called him at home this morning to set up an interview. This doesn't have anything to do with that steroids nonsense, does it?"

Lara charged down the stairs. "Dad, you didn't tell him anything about that, did you?"

"No. I thought we should keep that between you and me."

Thank God, Lara thought. But what would she tell her father the interview was about? She had tried to avoid lying to him up to this point, but desperate times called for desperate measures.

"Talk about coincidences," Lara said. "I call Coach Murdock right as he's going out to play golf with you."

"Imagine that. So what's the interview about?"

"Oh, nothing special. Just our usual preview of the wrestling season. James was supposed to set up the interview this week, but he forgot, so I did it for him today. We're getting close to deadline. The Coach didn't mind that I called him at home, did he?" Lara asked, feigning innocence.

"No, I don't think so. I think he was just a little surprised by the timing of the call," Dr. Crandall said, putting his clubs away in the hall closet.

Lara figured that as long as she was lying, she may as well tell a big one—one that would keep her father off her back for a while. "Dad, I've been thinking about what you said. You were right about the steroids investigation. I don't know what got into me. I've already forgotten about the whole thing."

"Well, I knew you would come to your senses, honey," her father said, sounding surprised by the turnaround. "So you're not going to harass the Coach tomorrow about some phantom steroids ring operating in the hallowed halls of Cresswell High?"

"I wouldn't dream of it," Lara said brightly, her fingers crossed behind her back.

Lara and James compared questions for the interview before journalism class on Monday morning. She was amazed at how many of her questions and James's questions were the same. They were definitely thinking along the same lines. That was a good sign.

During class, she gave James a note explaining what had happened with her father and the

Coach. He read it, then turned to her and pretended to mop sweat from his brow.

"CLOSE CALL!" he wrote in big letters on the back of the note, and held it up for her to read.

Mrs. Alexander saw them trading notes—*nothing* went by her unnoticed—but she didn't say anything about it. She just kept giving Lara and James wary looks. Normally, no one would have gotten away with passing notes in Mrs. Alexander's class. She was giving Lara and James a break because she knew the notes were about a potentially important story. Sometimes communication between two reporters working on a big story could come before the rules of a classroom. This was the kind of real-world lesson that was Mrs. Alexander's specialty.

After class, James walked Lara to her locker. "So, has Billy turned up yet?" he asked.

"I haven't seen him at school today, and his mother hasn't called our house to say he's come home, so I guess not," Lara replied.

"Did your father say anything to the Coach about Billy's disappearance?"

Lara knew she should have coaxed this bit of information out of her father, but she hadn't had the nerve. "I didn't find out. That whole conversation was so uncomfortable. I didn't want to prolong it."

"That's okay. We've got our first question for the interview: Where is Billy Owens?"

* * *

The red light on the tape recorder was lit, but dead silence fell on Murdock's office. "Pardon me?" the Coach said.

James repeated the question. "Where is Billy Owens?"

Coach Murdock laughed. "Who do I look like, the Amazing Kreskin? I heard that he wasn't in school, and he hasn't shown up for hockey practice yet. I guess he's home sick with the flu, along with half the Cresswell student body."

"He hasn't been seen since Friday," Lara informed the Coach.

The Coach seemed shocked by the news. "You're joking me."

James pressed on. "Are you saying that you have no idea where Billy Owens is right now?"

"Of course I don't," the Coach said, starting to lose his temper. "What are you getting at? If the boy is missing, the police will find him. And I'll do everything in my power to help them. I thought this interview was supposed to be about wrestling!"

Lara took the initiative. "It is. What do you know about possible steroid use among your wrestlers?" she asked.

The veins in Coach Murdock's neck popped out in anger. "All I know is one thing: my boys don't take them! If you want me to prove that to you, I'll be happy to test each and every one of them. They'll pass with flying colors!"

He reached across the desk and shut off the tape recorder. "Now get out of my office!"

James snatched the tape recorder off the desk and followed closely on Lara's heels as she scurried out the door. Coach Murdock slammed it behind them.

"Seems like we got the old boy's dander up," James said.

Lara was more shaken by his outburst. "Now I know what it feels like to be one of his wrestlers after losing a match."

James nodded in agreement. "He knows that we're onto him. Now we have to pin him down as the ringleader."

"That's easier said than done." Lara groaned. "We've still got a lot left to prove before Mrs. Alexander will let us print a word of this in the paper."

Chapter 8

Nick Glidden was sitting on a bench in the locker room putting on his skates for hockey practice as Lara and James interviewed Coach Murdock. Murdock's office door was open slightly, and the conversation carried. When Murdock raised his voice, Nick could hear every word crystal clear. The word "steroids" sent a chill down his spine.

Nick didn't use steroids. He didn't need to. He had been born with abundant athletic ability. With his gift for graceful skating and scoring, a bulky physique would only slow him down. College scouts were already talking to him about his future as a professional hockey player, and how their programs would help to assure it.

But Nick knew that the Evans boys had been taking steroids. He had seen the pills and syringes in their lockers. If they got caught, they would give the Cresswell High hockey team a bad reputation. Would scouts still want Nick then? They might not want to sign a player who had been linked even indirectly to steroids.

The Evanses and a few others had also shown up early for hockey practice. After Jake Powell and Frank Gibbons headed out onto the ice, Chuck and Chris suited up at their lockers against the far wall, uncharacteristically keeping to themselves. But when Coach Murdock's angry words echoed through the room—"I'll be happy to test each and every one of them"—Nick saw Chuck's head jerk up in attention.

Nick nonchalantly finished lacing his skate, then stood to leave, but Chuck pushed him back down on the bench. "You hearing any of this talk about steroids, Nick?" he asked, not-so-playfully tugging on Nick's blond ponytail.

"Is that what Coach Murdock is yelling about?" Nick asked. "I couldn't make out what had gotten him to fly off the handle this time."

Chuck wasn't buying Nick's hear-no-evil act, but he played along with it. "You don't know anything about steroids, do you, Nick?" He pulled harder on Nick's ponytail, snapping his head back.

"Not a thing," Nick said, gulping.

Chuck smiled and yanked Nick down to the locker-room floor. "And even if you did know something, you wouldn't tell anyone about it, would you?"

"Of course not. What good would that do me?" Nick said uneasily.

Chuck relinquished his death grip on Nick's ponytail. Nick's head rang with pain. "Glad to hear it," Chuck said, slapping Nick on the back. "Just checking." He and Chris stormed out into the rink.

Nick sat on the locker-room floor for a few minutes, wondering what to do. He had two choices—rat out the steroid users or keep his mouth shut. Both choices stunk.

During practice, Nick couldn't concentrate on his game. He didn't score once during the entire scrimmage, even though the pathetic second-string goalie, Felix Moss, filled in for Billy in the net. Out of the corner of his eye, Nick could see a college scout shaking his head, wondering what the big deal was about him. And Chuck Evans hassled Nick throughout the scrimmage, delivering ferocious body checks that rattled Nick's bones every time he skated into Chuck's zone.

By the end of practice, Nick was a physical and emotional wreck. He finally knew what he had to do: tell Lara and James about the Evanses' use of steroids. They were going to get to the bottom of it one way or another. Maybe being the whistle-blower would spare him from the scandal.

Nick steered clear of the Evans boys in the locker room after practice. Skipping a shower, he threw on his clothes and slammed out the door. He walked to a pay phone in the parking lot of the school. He thumbed nervously through the phone book that hung from a metal cord and found the listing for Dr. Warren Crandall. Nick dropped a quarter into the phone and dialed.

A girl answered. "Hello, is this Lara Crandall?" Nick asked, his voice quavering.

"Yes. Who is this?"

"I don't really know you, and I'm not sure you know who I am, but . . . My name is Nick Glidden. I'm a hockey player at Cresswell."

"Of course I know who you are," Lara said, her voice fluttering slightly. "What can I do for you?"

Nick paused and looked around him. The coast looked clear. "I need to talk to you about something. Something about the wrestling team. I think you know what I mean."

Lara's voice became more serious. "Yes, I do. Go on."

"Can you meet me at the hockey rink tonight, around midnight? I can show you physical evidence."

This was the break Lara had been waiting for. "I'll be there."

Nick hung up the phone. His heart was pounding. He started to walk home, his gaze fixed straight in front of him. He didn't notice that Chuck Evans, still in his uniform, was crouched behind a Pontiac next to the phone, listening to every word.

* * *

Lara was cooking dinner for her father when she got the call from Nick. Their argument had been resolved with Lara's lie about giving up on the story. Coach Murdock thankfully had not called her father to inform him about the content of the interview. All was well in the Crandall household.

"Who was that on the phone?" her father called from the living room after Lara put down the receiver.

"Wrong number," Lara lied again.

She wasn't about to tell her father that she had to leave the house at midnight to talk to a source. He wouldn't let her out of the house at that hour for any reason, much less for the steroids investigation.

Lara reveled in the excitement of it all. She felt like *Washington Post* reporter Bob Woodward arranging secret late-night meetings with his informant, "Deep Throat," to crack Watergate. Plus, the thought of being alone with Nick Glidden in a dark room late at night was in itself enough to get Lara's blood pumping.

She knew she would have to sneak out, but that wasn't much of a challenge. Her father was a pretty sound sleeper, and he was always in bed by eleven-thirty. Lara could barely sit still as the hours passed slowly after dinner.

Lara decided not to tell James about the meeting in advance. She could fill him in on all the details in the morning. Nick had called *her*, after all. He might clam up if she brought along someone else.

Eleven o'clock came, and Lara pretended to go to bed. She changed into her nightgown and went down to the living room to kiss her father good-night. He was dozing in the recliner, with the local news blaring on the TV. Lara shook him awake.

"I'm turning in," she said softly. "Maybe you should, too. You look like you're pretty beat."

"I'll come upstairs after the news. . . ." he mumbled, still half asleep.

Lara tried not to sound too insistent. "Dad, you're falling asleep in the middle of a sentence. Why don't you come to bed?"

"I'm okay. I'll come up soon," he mumbled.

Short of carrying him to bed—a hopeless proposition—there was nothing Lara could do. She hoped he would make it up to bed by midnight.

She went up to her room and changed back into her clothes. For the next hour, she lay under the covers and waited. The room was lit only by her digital clock radio, which she stared at helplessly. Until her father came upstairs, she was a virtual prisoner in her own house. Lara just hoped that Nick wouldn't give up and go home.

Nick looked at his digital watch as it flipped to 12:00 A.M. He stood alone at center ice of the dark rink. *What was keeping Lara?*

He had left one of the rink doors slightly ajar so she could get in. Maybe she hadn't figured that out and was waiting outside for him. He started walking toward the red Exit sign. Then he heard the sound of keys entering one of the doors to the rink. Someone was coming in!

The door opened, and harsh white light from the parking lot poured into the rink. A hulking figure entered the building. Nick couldn't tell who it was. He backed into the darkness, but slipped on the ice and fell.

Suddenly, the masked figure charged toward him on skates, carrying what looked like a hockey stick. "Lara, is that you?" Nick cried in panic, scrambling to get up off the ice.

"Guess again, traitor," growled the menacing skater as he began to cut furious circles around Nick on the ice, spraying him with ice shavings from his skates.

Nick tried to get up, but the skater's circles were slowly closing in on him; he was whizzing around Nick at what seemed to be a superhuman rate. It was like he was on every side of Nick at once.

The ice shavings flew up into Nick's eyes. In a flash it all became clear to him. There were two masked figures skating around him, not one. That's why the attacker seemed omnipresent.

Nick knew who he was dealing with: the Evans boys. Quickly he stuck out his foot, and the circle of terror was momentarily shattered. The tripped skater went crashing to the ice, and Nick recognized Chris from his childish cry of pain.

That left Chuck standing over Nick. In the dark, Nick couldn't quite make out the shape of the stick Chuck was hiding behind his back. It looked like Billy's goaltender stick, more compact and rounded than the other players' sticks.

Nick tried desperately to kick Chuck's left knee, remembering that Chuck had injured it in practice last week. But Chuck neatly evaded Nick's foot and slashed him hard in the face with his skate. Blood splattered onto the ice from the gash across Nick's forehead.

Streams of blood rushed over Nick's eyes, but he could see Chuck bringing the stick out from behind his back. Only Chuck wasn't wielding a goaltender's stick after all. It was a limb cutter! A glint of red light from the Exit sign reflected off the blades as Chuck slowly pulled the steel cable to open the blade.

Before Nick could scream, the blade snapped closed on his neck, severing his head from his body like a twig from a tree.

Chapter 9

Lara finally heard her father coming upstairs shortly after midnight. He opened her bedroom door a crack to check on her, as he had every night since she was a little girl. A sliver of white light from the hallway split the darkness of Lara's room. She closed her eyes tightly and breathed a sigh of relief when he shut the door.

She listened to him brushing his teeth in the bathroom and heard him shut his bedroom door behind him. Lara threw off her covers and grabbed her notebook and pencil. After tiptoeing out of her room, she creeped over to her father's bedroom door, hoping to hear his familiar snore.

He was dead to the world. Lara scurried downstairs and eased out the front door. It creaked as she shut it, but she knew it wouldn't be enough to wake her father.

Starting the car, however, would be another matter. Except for the sound of chirping crickets, Gaspee Farms was dead quiet at night. Revving the car engine underneath her father's bedroom window would be enough to wake him up. Lara had hoped to avoid this problem. If her father had gone to bed at eleven-thirty sharp, she would have had just enough time to walk the mile to school.

By now it was almost twelve-fifteen. Lara had no choice but to drive. She got into her Honda and fastened her seat belt, but didn't dare turn on the headlights. She gunned the engine once and backed out of the driveway as fast as she could.

She hesitated in front of the house for a second, switching into drive and flipping on her headlights. Her father suddenly appeared at his bedroom window. Lara's eyes locked with his for a moment, then she took off like a rocket down the street.

There was no turning back now. Her father had no idea where she was going, and she had too much of a head start for him to give chase. Lara knew there was going to be hell to pay when she got home, but she reminded herself that it would be worth it if Nick could help her break this story.

Lara made it to the school in record time. She sprang out of her car and ran to the rink doors, hoping that Nick was still waiting. She found the unlocked door and walked inside.

"Nick?" Lara called breathlessly into the darkness. There was no response. The room was pitch black, and she could barely see her hand in front of her face. Lara felt as though she had been struck blind. She carefully shuffled across the surface of the rink.

"Nick?" she said again, a little louder. All she heard was a hollow echo of her own voice. *Nick must have given up and gone home.* "Some reporter I am," she chided herself. "I miss a scoop because my dad won't let me out of the house. I bet this never happens to Sam Donaldson."

Lara turned around and walked toward the exit. When she opened the door, light from the parking lot poured into the rink. She turned around for one last look.

Lara spotted a slumped figure at center ice and started running cautiously across the ice toward it. The door slammed behind her, and she was enveloped in near-total darkness once again.

She skidded to a slippery stop in front of the bundled heap. She stared at it uncomprehendingly for a moment. It couldn't be. But it was. It was Nick's headless body. Lara gasped—she was too scared to scream—and looked down at her feet. She was standing in a pool of blood.

Lara stepped back from the body, dumbstruck with terror. She began backpedaling rapidly, leaving a trail of bloody shoeprints on the ice. She tripped over something and fell, cracking her head against the hard ice.

As Lara lay semiconscious, she saw the object that had tripped her spinning slowly in a circle toward her. Nick's head, the eyes and mouth frozen open, rolled to a stop right next to Lara. Lara tasted the vomit welling up in her mouth, then everything went black.

The first thing Lara saw when she opened her eyes was her father standing over her. Then a bright white light blinded her.

"Is this your daughter?" Officer Hendrikson said, shining his high-powered flashlight directly on Lara's face.

Dr. Crandall dropped to his knees next to Lara. "Honey, can you hear me?" he asked.

For a second, Lara couldn't remember where she was, then it all came racing back to her. "Yes," she whispered hoarsely.

"Can you move?"

Aside from a ringing headache and a cold numbness from lying on the ice, Lara wasn't suffering any physical pain. She sat up on the ice, still in a daze.

The piercing wail of ambulance sirens approaching the school made Lara's head hurt worse. "Are you okay? Do you want me to take you to the hospital?" her father said above the noise.

"No," Lara answered without even thinking.

"Let me check you out," her father insisted. He began to examine her for a concussion. Lara sat silently.

Two paramedics rushed into the dark rink.

Officer Hendrikson shined his flashlight on them and said, "Slow down, boys. We've got one DOA and one who's being checked out. Can one of you find the lights in this place?"

One of the paramedics searched for the light switches as the other helped Dr. Crandall examine Lara. Officer Hendrikson stood over Nick's body, waiting for department detectives to arrive.

Dr. Crandall and the paramedics agreed that Lara didn't need medical attention. After giving Officer Hendrikson a brief statement about how she discovered the body, she asked if she could go home.

"I just have one more question," Hendrikson said. "Why were you supposed to meet the deceased here tonight?"

Lara looked at her father for a moment. "Answer the officer's question," he said.

Trying to gather her rushing thoughts, Lara started to recount the steroids story as she knew it. Officer Hendrikson took notes, occasionally nodding. Dr. Crandall listened quietly, shaking his head in disgust.

Dr. Crandall didn't say much as he helped Lara get into his car. "What about my car?" she asked.

"I'll come and get it tomorrow, honey. You're in no condition to drive," her father explained as he turned the key in the ignition.

Lara knew she should apologize to her father

for lying, but she couldn't quite muster the words. "I guess you're pretty mad at me," was all she could say.

"I am upset," her father corrected her, "but I can't be mad at you right now. I'm too glad that you're alive to be mad at you. You put yourself in a lot of danger tonight."

"I know, but I had to follow up on this lead," Lara said. "Can't you see now that there *is* something going on with steroids at Cresswell? It's much more serious than even I thought. *Somebody* didn't want Nick to talk about it!"

"Oh, Lara, you're still not fixated on this steroids thing, are you? I let you speak your piece to Officer Hendrikson because it was that cockamamie investigation that brought you down to the rink in the first place. But I really don't think it has any bearing on the murder."

Lara couldn't believe that her father was still skeptical. "Who do you think killed Nick?" she asked.

"Some sicko maniac, judging from what he did to the kid. Maybe there's some nutcase running around Cresswell killing kids. Maybe he got Billy, too, and we haven't found out about it yet. But there is no reason to believe this is part of some steroids conspiracy!"

"Then why did Nick want to talk to me tonight?"

"Lara, teenage boys will use any excuse to get alone with a pretty girl. Nick probably heard about your little story and tried to use it to lure you down here for God knows what. I mean, I never knew the kid when he was alive, but he could have been a real playboy—"

"Dad!" Lara cut him off. "I'm sorry for lying, okay? But I'm not going to drop the steroids story. You may not believe it, but I know that I'm onto something very big here."

They rode the rest of the way home in silence. Before Dr. Crandall could even turn off the engine, Lara had jumped out of the car and run into the house. Her father got his medical bag out of the car and followed close behind.

Lara stormed up the stairs and threw herself onto her bed. Dr. Crandall came in and sat down next to her. Lara stiffened and prepared herself for yet another bedside diagnosis.

"Lara, you're having delusions. This doesn't mean that you're crazy. Let me explain. Sometimes the mind plays tricks on you when it's overwhelmed. You were under stress applying to colleges, then you weren't sleeping because of your nightmares, and now there's a killer terrorizing your friends. That's a lot for a little girl to handle."

"Dad, I'm not a little girl!" Lara reminded him angrily.

"I'm going to give you a sedative now. This will help you sleep." Dr. Crandall pulled a needle out of his bag.

"Dad, no!" Lara resisted, but her father

grabbed her arm and deftly injected the sedative. Very quickly Lara felt weak, and then the room darkened and faded away.

Lara felt herself falling into the nightmare again. Even though it was always the same dream, it never failed to scare Lara. She saw her mother's head hanging by a string of flesh from her body. Only, in this dream, when Lara looked down it was Nick's head that was staring up at her. And this time Lara couldn't wake herself up by screaming.

Chapter 10

The sedative wore off late the next morning. Lara woke up and was relieved to find herself safe in her room. She had been terrified of being trapped forever in the haunted house of her subconscious mind.

Her head throbbed with pain. Instinctively, Lara reached over for her notebook on the nightstand to jot down what she remembered about last night's events. Then she saw the clock and panicked—it was ten o'clock, and she was late for school.

She jumped out of bed to get dressed, her mind racing with thoughts. Would they even hold school today? Would they announce Nick's death? How would the students react to the news? She was missing out on events that were vital to the breaking story.

She flung open the door to her room and ran downstairs. Tacked on the back of the front door was a note from her father. Lara almost didn't stop to read it, but she saw the first line: "DON'T GO TO SCHOOL!"

"Sorry to leave you alone, but I had to go to work," the note continued. "I made an appointment for you this afternoon with Dr. Walter Lorenzo, the chief of psychiatry at the hospital. *THIS DOESN'T MEAN THAT YOU'RE CRAZY!* Please meet me at my office at noon. We'll have lunch and discuss this more. Love, Dad."

Lara crumpled up the note and drove to school in a rush. She parked illegally in the teacher's lot and hurried into the building. Third period had just begun, and Lara raced down the hall toward Mrs. Alexander's room.

She opened the door to the room and heard Mrs. Walters, the principal, making an announcement on the loudspeaker. Some of the students were crying, and Mrs. Alexander sat pensively behind her desk. No one seemed to notice Lara standing in the doorway.

The announcement continued: "Police are advising students to avoid school grounds at night. They are also urging anyone with information about this case to come forward. Funeral services for Nicholas Glidden will be held tomorrow at eleven A.M. at Greenbrier United Methodist Church. The school will be closed for the rest of today and tomorrow so that we can all deal with our grief. Classes will resume Thursday morning, and counselors will be available for anyone who would like to discuss his or her feelings."

The announcement ended, but no one got up

to leave. Except for the sound of students quietly sobbing, dead silence fell over the room. Lara walked over to her desk and sat down. James looked at her helplessly, his eyes filled with confusion.

Mrs. Alexander rose from her chair and addressed the class. "This is a very sad day for all of us," she began. "For many of you, this may be the first time someone you know has passed away. This is an especially difficult loss, both because of Nick's youth and the manner in which he died. I urge you all to attend the funeral and to utilize the counseling service. I'll see you all on Thursday."

With that, Mrs. Alexander left the room. The students began filing out of the room one by one. Lara and James stayed seated at their desks until they were alone.

"Do you know anything about this?" James asked.

Lara didn't know where to begin. "I discovered the body."

James's eyes popped open. "You're kidding!"

"I wish I were," Lara said, then blurted out the whole story. When she was finished, James reached out and took her hand.

"I'm really sorry you had to go through all that. I wish you had called me before you went to meet Nick, but I understand why you had to go alone. I take it that you think Nick's murder has something to do with the steroids."

"Yes," Lara said simply.

"Are you too scared to keep working on the story?" James asked. "The police know all about it now. We could leave it up to them."

"I'm not scared," Lara said, her voice trembling. "Are you?"

James hesitated for a second. "A little, but I don't think we should give up. It's more important than ever that we get to the bottom of this."

Lara was glad to hear it. "What should we do next?" she asked.

"I'm going to hit some more pharmacies to see if anyone has seen anything. I think we should both go to the funeral tomorrow. You never know—the killer could show up."

"You've been watching too many reruns of *Quincy*," Lara said, smiling weakly. "I'm going to stop by Billy's house today and see if his mother has heard from him."

"You're going down into the Lower Basin alone?"

"You sound like my dad!" Lara exclaimed. She was determined to confront her deep-seated fear of the neighborhood. "It's not like I'm going to Beirut or the South Bronx or something. I'll be fine."

"Maybe I should go with you," James said.

"No, no. I need to do this by myself." James bit his lip, then seemed to come to a decision. "Suit yourself," he said. "But be careful."

"I will. I'll call you tonight, okay?"

Lara walked out into the hallway. Most of the students hadn't left the building yet. Lara noticed that several of her classmates were staring at her and whispering as she walked by. Had the word that Lara had discovered Nick's body gotten around the school already?

She decided to ignore them. Suddenly, someone stuck out his foot in front of her, and Lara tripped and fell, her books scattering on the floor.

Lara looked up and saw the Evans twins standing over her. "Oops," Chuck said unconvincingly.

Chris started to gather up Lara's books for her, and Chuck slapped him hard across the back of the head. Chris yelped in pain and retreated to a bank of lockers.

"Watch where you're going next time, you oaf!" Lara said.

"Yeah, I wouldn't want anyone to get hurt," Chuck said belligerently. "But when you don't watch your step, sometimes you end up taking a fall. Know what I mean?"

"You're so philosophical!" Lara picked up her books and headed out the door.

She drove down into the Lower Basin and hunted for Billy's house. She had gotten the street address from the phone book, but she was unfamiliar with the neighborhood and got lost several times. Creepy-looking guys lurked on the street corners. Lara tried to ignore them. She didn't dare ask them for directions.

Finally, she found the Owens house. It was the dingiest, most run-down house on the block. Although the lawn was neatly mowed, the house itself was little more than a shack. Lara parked in front of it, locked her door, and walked up to the front door.

She hoped that Mrs. Owens wasn't at work. Billy mentioned that his mother sometimes worked the night shift at the diner, so Lara thought she would probably be home during the day. She pushed the doorbell, then knocked.

Mrs. Owens came running to the door. She opened it, looking frenzied at first, then disappointed, then confused. "Can I help you?" she finally said.

Lara hadn't thought that Mrs. Owens might not recognize her. It had been almost ten years since she had seen her. The years had not been kind to Mrs. Owens. She looked tired, wrinkled, and much older than Lara's father.

"Hello, Mrs. Owens," Lara said warmly. "It's Lara Crandall. Sorry to stop by without calling."

Mrs. Owens's face brightened. "Why, Lara, it's been years! Come in, won't you?"

Lara stepped inside. The living room looked like a disaster area. Mrs. Owens cleared newspapers and clothing off one of the chairs, and Lara took a seat.

"I just stopped by to see if you had heard anything from Billy," Lara said uncomfortably.

Mrs. Owens's face crumbled once again. "Billy? No. I filed a report with the police yesterday, and they said they would look for him. I have no idea where he is."

"He didn't say anything to you?" Lara asked.

"No. Nothing," Mrs. Owens said, looking down at the floor. "The police think he ran away from home, and that he'll come back once he realizes how hard it is to survive on the street."

"Do you believe that?" Lara asked hesitantly.

Mrs. Owens fought back tears. "Oh, I don't know. I haven't been able to provide much of a family life for Billy these past ten years. . . . I certainly wouldn't blame him for being unhappy. I'm unhappy, too, but I can't just run away from it like that." She broke down crying.

Lara didn't want to suggest that Billy might not have run away. Mrs. Owens believed he would come back, and Lara knew that might be the only thing that was keeping her going right now.

"I'm sorry," Mrs. Owens said through her tears.

"That's okay," Lara tried to console her. "I know how hard this must be on you. Is there anything my father or I can do to help out?"

Mrs. Owens snapped to attention with that remark. Her tone became bitter. "No, thank you. Your family has done quite enough for us.

All you can do to help me right now is to leave me alone."

Lara did just that. Her visit to Billy's mother had been a complete failure, both from a personal and a journalistic standpoint. Instead of finding out the truth, it seemed as if Lara was just making everything more confused.

Chapter 11

Against her father's wishes, Lara went to Nick's funeral the next day. She and James arrived at the church early, but the parking lot was already jammed with cars.

"Looks like it's going to be a full house," James said.

"Nick was a popular guy," Lara reminded him as she pulled into what looked like the only spot left in the lot.

She turned off the engine and reached for her notebook on the back seat. "Do you think it's disrespectful to take notes at a funeral?" she asked James.

James shook his head. "No, not if you're covering it for the paper. You don't want to misquote Coach Murdock's eulogy—especially after the tongue-lashing he gave us the other day."

"Good point." She grabbed an extra pencil.

They walked toward the entrance to the church, passing several tight clusters of students standing in the parking lot. As Lara passed, conversations halted. The news had spread that she had discovered the body.

Lara tried to ignore the stares and whispers, but Kim Marsh stepped out in front of her. "What are you doing here?" she demanded.

"The same thing you're doing, going to Nick's funeral." She tried to step around Kim.

"Leave her alone, Kim," James said.

Kim directed her venom toward James. "Who are you, her boyfriend? Better be careful. She made mine disappear."

"And you sound really broken up about it," Lara said. Kim grappled for words as Lara and James walked into the church.

Almost all the pews were filled, with students, teachers, and members of the community. Lara and James walked to the front of the church searching for seats. The sound of whispering followed Lara up the aisle.

Lara shuddered when she saw the open casket next to the altar. *How did they get Nick's head back on?* She and James squeezed into the end of the second row.

"Are you okay?" James whispered as the organist began playing.

"I'm fine," Lara replied. "You think I'm going to let a jerk like Kim upset me? No way."

Nick's family walked in and took their seats in front of James and Lara. They were the only people in the church who didn't seem to notice Lara's presence.

The minister opened the service with a reading from the Bible, then said a few words about Nick's participation in the church's youth sports league. After a hymn, the minister introduced Coach Murdock for the eulogy.

Murdock stepped up to the podium. He was dressed in a conservative dark suit. It was the first time Lara had ever seen him without a whistle around his neck. She opened her notebook and poised her pencil.

"Nick Glidden was more than just a great hockey player," the Coach said. "He was a great human being. You've heard the minister speak about his involvement with programs here at his church. I'm here to tell you about the contribution he made to his school."

Lara frantically scribbled every word. "Nick was one of the most well-liked boys at Cresswell. You can tell that from the overwhelming turnout of the student body here today." The Coach gestured out toward the overflowing crowd. Lara turned and looked at the throng of young people packed in behind her. Tears were rolling down many of their faces.

She noticed that the members of the hockey team in attendance were all sitting together in one row, eyeballing each other cautiously to see if anyone was crying. The only players from the squad absent were Billy and the Evans boys. Lara took note of this in the margin of the page, then caught up with Murdock's speech.

"Nick Glidden wasn't well-liked because he was handsome. He wasn't well-liked because he was a great hockey player or an above-average student or a natural leader, though he was all of these things. Nick was well-liked because he was a genuine, kind, and decent person."

Lara froze when she looked up and saw the Coach staring directly at her. "It was refreshing in this day and age to have known such a pure-souled young man. So many of today's teenagers seem to be irresponsible individuals interested only in making trouble and questioning the integrity of their elders."

James grabbed Lara's pencil and wrote on the top of the notebook page: "You think he means us?" Lara nodded and kept on writing.

"But now Nick has been taken away from us. He'll never score another goal for my team—the home team—Cresswell High. But I take comfort in knowing that he has gone to a better place," the Coach said, his voice cracking with emotion. "Because his goals in life were always more important to him than his goals on the ice."

Lara closed her notebook as Coach Murdock stepped down from the podium. The service continued, and finally the minister allowed everyone to file past the coffin to pay their last respects.

"Should we get in line?" James asked.

"I suppose so," she said, getting up.

They stood in silence as the line inched forward. Finally, Lara got close enough to see inside the casket. The gash on Nick's forehead had been closed up, and his head had been sewn back onto his body with thick black thread. Lara could see the stitches peeking out from under Nick's shirt collar. She felt faint and walked woozily down the center aisle toward the exit.

James caught up with Lara and put his arm around her waist to steady her. "Are you sure you're okay?" he asked.

Lara was white as a ghost. "I'll be fine. Did you see what they did? Why couldn't they just have had a closed casket?"

"It must have been his family's decision," James said. "Some people want to see them for one last time. Seeing the body makes it easier for them to deal with the loss."

Lara didn't understand. She had seen her mother's lifeless body, and it hadn't helped her "deal with the loss." In fact, the vision of her mother's corpse haunted her. Many times she had wished that her mother could have died in some other way, at some other time, when Lara couldn't have witnessed it.

Kim stood in the lobby huddled with some of her cheerleader friends as Lara and James walked out of the sanctuary together. "My, what a cute couple!" Kim said acidly. "And what a romantic first date! What next, kids? Cruise the highway looking for auto accidents?"

James dropped his arm. "She felt faint," he said.

"Whatever for?" Kim mocked her. "I heard you saw Nick in a much less presentable state the other night at the rink."

"Where did you hear that?" Lara demanded.

"Word gets around. *Everybody* knows you were the one to discover the body."

"Drop dead," Lara said, and James dragged her out to the parking lot.

"I thought you said you weren't going to let her upset you," James reminded her.

Lara shrugged. "I lied."

James looked at his watch. "Listen, there's a pharmacy around the corner that I haven't checked out yet. I'm going to head over there now. Can you make it home without me?"

"Sure," Lara said. "Give me a call if you find out anything."

"Will do. But they're probably going to give me the same old rap about confidentiality—they haven't seen anything, and even if they have, they couldn't tell me about it." James waved and set off for McCarthy's Drugs.

Old Man McCarthy was stooped over, sweeping the sidewalk in front of his store, when James walked up. James knew it would do no good to ask him anything. To him, all kids looked the same—and were the same. They all wanted to steal his candy, and it was his mission in life to stop them.

James didn't even go near the candy aisle when he walked inside. He walked straight back to the prescription counter, which was being manned by Ernie Zeff, one of his classmates.

Ernie smiled when he saw James approaching. "James, what brings you here?"

"I was in the neighborhood. At Nick's funeral." Ernie was kind of a nerd, but James had always gotten along pretty well with him. They had met in freshman gym, where they had been the two most consistently uncoordinated guys in class. Ernie worshiped James because he was the only remotely cool person in school who even spoke to him.

"Yeah, I wanted to go, but the old geezer offered me an extra shift here and I really needed the money. How was it?"

James searched for the right words. "Pretty creepy."

"I bet. Did a lot of people show up?"

"Everybody who is anybody in Cresswell."

"I bet. So did they catch the killer yet?"

James lowered his voice to a whisper. "I'm working on it."

Ernie laughed. *"You're* working on it?"

James shushed Ernie. "Yeah. That's what brings me here."

"Huh?"

"I can't tell you much, but I need to know if

you've seen any Cresswell athletes coming in to pick up prescriptions."

Ernie scratched his head. "No. Old Man McCarthy usually chases all the kids out the store with his broom."

James gave Ernie a knowing look. "Hey, man, I know about the confidentiality thing. You couldn't tell me anything even if you knew something, right?"

"No way, man. I'd tell you. I just don't know anything. All I do around here is run the cash register, and I may not even get to do that much longer. The old man accused me of stealing pennies!"

James laughed. Ernie was the most honest guy he knew. "Thanks anyway, man. But keep an eye out for me, will you?"

"Sure thing," Ernie said. "Hey, who are you working with on this case, the cops?"

"No way." James paused. He knew Ernie would be jealous; he had a crush on Lara, too. "Lara Crandall."

"Wow, she's hot!" Ernie said.

"She's outta your league, pal," James kidded him.

"I see her dad in here all the time," Ernie said.

This was news. "Really? They don't live around here. I wonder why he comes here instead of going to Gruber's."

"I don't know, but he picks up his patients' prescriptions here a couple times a week."

A doctor picking up his patients' prescriptions? James's mind raced. "What are the prescriptions for?"

"I dunno," Ernie admitted. "But they sure are expensive."

James took a deep breath. "What I'm about to ask you to do could cost you your job, so I'll understand if you say no."

"Run it by me. I owe you one from freshman gym when you saved me from getting beaten up by Chuck Evans."

"Can you find out what those prescriptions were for?"

Ernie thought for a moment. "I'll have to get the keys to the file drawers." He straightened up. "Meet me behind the store in five minutes."

James slipped past Old Man McCarthy on his way out the door.

"You didn't steal any of my candy, did you, you little punk?" McCarthy called after him.

"Who, me?" James said. "No, sir."

"Keep it that way," he snarled.

James waited impatiently behind the store, tapping his foot against the pavement and checking his watch every other minute. Finally, Ernie emerged from the employees' exit with some papers.

"Here you go, man. Read it and weep," he said.

James couldn't believe his eyes. Every single one of the prescriptions, stretching back over two months, was for anabolic steroids. All of them were prescribed and paid for by Dr. Crandall.

"Thanks," James muttered, handing the papers back to Ernie. "You'd better get these back in the files."

"No problem. Let me know if I can do anything else."

"Just keep quiet about the whole thing."

"Mum's the word," Ernie said.

James stumbled down the block. The culprit had been right under Lara's nose the whole time. But how could he tell her that her father was the supplier? The steroids investigation had brought James and Lara closer together; his hopeless longing for her looked as if it might finally grow into romance. James hoped that, unlike the ancient Greeks, Lara wouldn't kill the messenger bearing bad news.

Chapter 12

Billy had been hiding out in the woods for five days. His Boy Scout training had served him well. He had managed to cut his hands free with his pocketknife while he was underwater. After swimming to the surface of the lake, he sat on the shore, gathering his thoughts and catching his breath. He decided to stay out in the woods for a while, giving himself time to recuperate and plot his return to Cresswell.

With the use of natural salves and leaf bandages, his head wounds had healed. He found plants and roots to eat, fished, and drank lake water, which he boiled over a campfire.

He could have survived alone out there for weeks, if it weren't for one thing that he craved: steroids. When he had started taking them, Billy thought there was no way he could get hooked; he thought he could stop taking them anytime he wanted. Now that he didn't have any, he felt as though he was going to die. He needed them, and would do anything to get them.

There were no mirrors out in the woods, but

Billy looked at his reflection in the surface of the rippling lake and imagined that he could see his physique deteriorating before his eyes. He constantly squeezed his biceps and triceps to see if they were softening. He did push-ups and sit-ups obsessively to try to retain his muscle tone, but in his mind, there seemed to be no way to halt the withering of his massive bulk.

Billy wondered if he was hallucinating or if his body actually was shrinking. He hadn't slept much; he knew that insomnia played tricks on the mind. His nonstop craving for the drugs clouded his thinking even more. Was this reality that he was experiencing, or was he losing his mind from a combination of sleep deprivation and addiction withdrawal?

He hadn't spoken to another human being in five days. "I'm not crazy," Billy would say out loud, listening to make sure he could still hear the sound of his own voice. "I don't need the drugs." But all that he wanted and all he thought about was steroids—and how to get them soon.

Dr. Crandall had always gotten the drugs for him, but before dinner on Friday night he had begged Billy to stop taking them. "You've got to stop. Lara's onto us," Dr. Crandall whispered as his daughter fixed dinner in the other room. The words echoed in Billy's mind. "Lara's onto us."

Lara Crandall. *She has it all.* A rich father, a nice house, a car of her own, good looks, good grades, her pick of colleges. She had a future. What did Billy have? His muscles, and not a whole lot more. If he pumped up to give himself a better future, what business was it of Lara's? She said she was his friend, but he wondered if she meant it. Maybe she had been nice to him all these years because she felt guilty about the accident. Now she was ready to ruin him to get a scoop for the school paper. Some friend.

She's a chip off the old block, Billy thought. He never forgot that it was her father who had been driving that night. The courts said that it wasn't Dr. Crandall's fault, and maybe it wasn't. The other driver was drunk, it was dark, and the roads were slippery. No one could blame Dr. Crandall for what happened. But the crash had demolished Billy's life, and he felt that somebody should make it up to him.

When Billy had decided that steroids could give him the chance at a college scholarship, he needed to find a doctor who could get them for him. Dr. Crandall was the natural choice. The man who had taken away his future could give it back to him again with the simple stroke of a pen.

Now it had all gone wrong. "Lara's onto us." Us: you, me, and the Evans twins. Chuck had seen Billy sneaking the drugs out of his locker one day, and blackmailed him into getting them for him and his brother, too. Chuck had threatened to turn Billy in if he didn't get them, so

Billy threatened to turn in Dr. Crandall if he didn't provide enough steroids for the three of them.

Chuck had become a monster on the drugs—even more brutish and erratic in his behavior than before. His paranoid fury had escalated until he was convinced that Billy was going to blow the whistle on him to Lara. Then had come the attack, and Billy was left to die in the lake.

Billy sat on the ground with his head buried between his knees, thinking out loud about the Evanses and the Crandalls. "None of them cares about me. They all deserve to die. They still think they have a future. But I can take it away."

First he needed to get steroids to shore up his strength. He could break into the Evanses' gym lockers and steal theirs. They were so stupid, they didn't even carry the drugs with them. Without their stash, where would they be? They could shrivel up and die, for all Billy cared. Dr. Crandall wouldn't get them any more. "Lara's onto us."

Billy looked up at the sun. It was about four in the afternoon. By the time he made it to school, hockey practice would be over. He still had his key to the gym. He could sneak in, find the drugs, and take them. Then, restored to full strength, he could stalk his prey and wreak his bloody vengeance.

* * *

Billy jogged the five miles of winding roads that led to the school, nervously looking over his shoulder whenever cars passed. He had been missing for five days—had they shown his picture on the news yet? Billy imagined his face emblazoned on the side of milk cartons: *Have you seen this boy? Do you care?* Billy wondered if his mother was worried about him, or just relieved to have him out of her hair for once.

In his weakened condition, Billy felt exhausted by the time he made it to the school shortly after dark. The lights were turned off in the gym, and Billy, still gasping for breath, unlocked the door and walked warily inside. The place seemed deserted, except for the sound of clanking iron from the weight room at the far end of the gym.

Someone had stayed late after hockey practice to work out. Billy couldn't get into the locker room next door without attracting their attention. He crept up to the door of the weight room and peered inside.

Chuck and Chris were pumping iron. This was too good to be true. He didn't even have to go looking for his victims. They were lying next to each other on benches, facing away from him. Chuck lifted a barbell above his head over and over again. Chris was using the resistance system, pulling to his chest handles that were connected by a pulley to a stack of weights behind his head. Other weights and dumbbells littered

112

the floor. Billy crouched next to the doorway, out of sight, and listened in on the brothers' angry conversation.

"I don't know about this stuff, man," Chris grunted as he struggled to match Chuck repetition for repetition.

Chuck pumped his barbell faster. "You don't know about *what?*" he said in a strong, clear voice.

Chris gave up trying to keep pace with Chuck and crossed his bulging arms on his heaving chest. "This whole thing. You told me we weren't going to kill anybody."

Chuck continued his ferocious lifting. "I lied."

Billy grinned. They thought he was dead. They were about to receive the surprise of their lives.

"I know you didn't mean to kill Billy. That just happened. But what was the deal with that limb cutter the other night? I thought we were just going to rough Nick up."

"So did Nick," Chuck said, chortling.

Billy drew back quickly and felt violently sick to his stomach. They had killed Nick! They were animals. These maniacs had to be stopped before they killed again.

Chris started to cry. "I don't want to be a killer, Chuck," he blubbered.

Chuck angrily slammed his barbell onto the iron stand over his head. He leaped up from the bench and jumped on top of Chris, landing on his chest. "What are you talking about?" he screamed in Chris's contorted face.

Chris was hysterical. "I'm going to turn myself in to the police and tell them the truth. I didn't kill anybody. You're the killer!" he blurted out.

Chuck's beefy hands encircled Chris's neck, choking him, savagely clutching his windpipe. "You're right about that," he growled as he watched his twin brother's face turn purplish red.

Billy looked on in helpless glee. His job was being done for him. The Evans boys were going to kill each other.

Chris kicked his feet violently, trying to shake his brother off him. Chuck smiled maniacally as he felt the last breath about to slip from his brother's body. Chris stretched his arms out to his sides, his fingers turning gray, grasping for life.

With his last spurt of strength, he picked up a ten-pound dumbbell from the floor next to him and smashed Chuck in the head with it. The force of the blow knocked Chuck off, and Chris struggled to sit up, wheezing for breath. With a confused expression, Chuck collapsed slowly on the floor, a pool of blood spreading out behind his blond head.

Billy ducked out of sight. Chris sat on the bench, his hands clasped to his throat. "Oh, my

God!" he cried hoarsely at the sight of his brother's lifeless body. "I *am* a killer! I am!"

Chris staggered to his feet and bolted out of the weight room. In his shock, he ran right past Billy without seeing him. Billy didn't give chase. If Chris turned himself in to the police, Billy's work would be half done. The Evans boys' futures would be destroyed: Chris would be in jail and Chuck would burn in hell. He listened as Chris charged through the gym doors and kept on running.

Billy smiled, then burst out laughing. He felt powerful again, as if he had been able to will the Evans boys to attack each other. He could control their destinies with his mind. He didn't even need to use his tremendous physical strength to get his retribution.

He walked into the locker room and raided both brothers' lockers. It was no problem to bust the flimsy combination locks. They didn't have much left—it had been almost a week since Dr. Crandall's last drop—but it would be enough to keep him going. He popped some of Chris's pills, then stuffed Chuck's needles and serum into his coat pocket along with one of the broken locks.

He felt a rush of rage and power sweep through his body. "I'm coming to get you, Lara!" he yelled at the top of his lungs. He dropped to the floor and did a quick twenty push-ups, then ran out to the gym, screaming out the school fight song.

He paused and looked up at the championship banner. His mind flashed back to the last practice. "I can fly!" he roared. "I can will people to die! I can do *anything!* I am the champion of the world!"

Inside Billy's head, he could hear the whole school cheering him on as he ran out the door and headed for the Crandalls' house. "Billy, Billy, he's our man, if he can't do it, nobody can. . . ."

Chapter 13

Lara was home alone. Her father was working late at the hospital again, so she fixed herself dinner. She took her meal into the living room and sat down in front of the TV.

Lara flipped the channels restlessly, searching for something that would take her mind off the investigation for a little while. The funeral had upset her—Kim's attack, Nick's body in the open casket, and the knowledge that the murderer might still be walking the streets of Cresswell.

She settled on channel 7 and *Entertainment Tonight*. The opening teaser promised an interview with Tom Cruise and a special report about the racy content of TV sitcoms—nothing that could possibly remind Lara of the steroids case. But as she leaned back and took a drink of Diet Pepsi, the program was interrupted by a special bulletin from the local news team.

"Great," Lara said. "I miss Tom Cruise to hear the latest details on the Gorby Victory Tour."

"This is an Eyewitness News special report," the newscaster said. "I'm Ted Bishop."

"Hi, Ted," Lara said sarcastically. "What's up? Gorby's coming to the mall?"

She choked on her drink when the next image appeared on the screen. It was Chris Evans's junior yearbook picture. "Cresswell police report that they have apprehended Christopher Gordon Evans, an eighteen-year-old senior at Cresswell High, in connection with the murders of his twin brother Charles and his classmate Nicholas Glidden, and the disappearance and suspected murder of another student, William Randolph Owens."

Lara stared in disbelief as Billy's old yearbook picture flashed across the screen. As she listened for the rest of the details, she reached for the phone to notify James. Just then she felt hot breath on her neck and an eerie shadow fell over the sofa. Turning around, Lara screamed. Billy was standing behind her, looking bigger, stronger, and angrier than the picture on the television.

Lara stood up and backed away from him. "Billy! You're alive! You scared me."

"I meant to," he said softly, walking toward her.

Lara was frightened. *What does he want? Where has he been?* She tried to stall for time to think. "I'm so glad you're okay."

"Are you?" He backed her into a corner.

The TV blared on. "Police will drag the lake tomorrow searching for the body of Owens . . ."

Lara panicked when she saw Billy pull out his pocketknife. "You're coming with me," he said calmly, taking hold of her arm.

"Where are we going?" she asked frantically.

"I'm taking you over to my house. I promise I won't use this if you come quietly," Billy said, gesturing with the knife.

Lara believed him. She had no choice.

James had sat alone in his room all day, thinking over the situation. He wanted to call Lara and tell her what he had found out about her father, but he couldn't bring himself to do it.

After dinner, he finally decided what to do. He would confront Dr. Crandall with the evidence and see what he had to say for himself. Maybe there was some explanation. Maybe he was being blackmailed or something. James didn't want to destroy Lara's love for her father before he knew all the details.

He felt guilty for not telling Lara everything he knew right away, but he remembered that she hadn't informed him about Nick's phone call when it happened. Sometimes a reporter working on a story had to keep a partner in the dark for a while, for the good of the investigation. It was one of Mrs. Alexander's famous paradoxes: "As a reporter, you must always remember that you work for a news organization, but when in the pursuit of a story, you must sometimes isolate yourself from your colleagues."

James tried to call Dr. Crandall at home. He had his finger poised to hang up in case Lara answered. There was no one home. It was almost eight o'clock. Was he still working? *And where is Lara?*

James dialed the number of the hospital and asked if Dr. Crandall was in his office. The receptionist said he was but he had left orders not to be disturbed. James thanked her, hung up the phone, went out to his car, and drove to the hospital.

This is the perfect setup, James thought. *I'll get him alone in his office and spring it on him. If he's the killer, he can't do anything to me there. Maybe he'll break down and spill his guts. Just don't let him leave before I get there.*

James double-parked his car outside the emergency-room entrance and sprinted inside. The admitting nurse flagged him down. "Excuse me, young man, this is the *emergency* room. What do you think you're doing parking out there?"

"This *is* an emergency," James said. "Where is Dr. Warren Crandall's office?"

"May I ask what this is concerning?" the nurse demanded.

James said the first thing that came into his head. "His daughter is in a lot of danger!"

The nurse pointed down the hall. "It's all the way at the end of this corridor. Room 119."

James took off down the hall. He knocked quickly on the door to Room 119, then opened the door. Dr. Crandall looked up from the papers on his desk, obviously alarmed. "What's the meaning of this intrusion? Who are you?" he bellowed.

Closing the office door behind him, James gathered his thoughts. "My name is James Horton. I'm a friend of your daughter's."

Dr. Crandall looked concerned. "Is there something wrong? Is Lara okay?"

"She's fine," James explained. "I work with her on the newspaper at school. . . ."

"This isn't more of that steroids nonsense, is it?"

James took a deep breath. "It's not nonsense, Dr. Crandall. You know it's not nonsense, and I know it's not nonsense. I have evidence proving that you prescribed steroids through Mc-Carthy's pharmacy to Billy Owens and the Evans brothers."

"This is absurd. . . ." Dr. Crandall reached for his intercom. "Get out of my office, or I'll have you thrown out!"

"I have copies of the prescriptions you wrote," James bluffed.

Dr. Crandall blanched. He was caught. "Well, now. W-w-what are you planning on doing with thom?"

James couldn't think of a good answer to that. "Frankly, I don't know yet. I thought I would give you a chance to explain before I told the police—and Lara."

"It wasn't my idea," Dr. Crandall said, the sweat beading on his forehead. "Billy Owens asked me to help him obtain steroids. Foolishly I did, out of guilt over something that happened many years ago. I knew it was wrong, and I tried to get him to stop. Then he got the Evans boys in on it. He was completely hooked, and he threatened to ruin my career if I didn't continue cooperating. I couldn't let that happen. Not just for my sake. For Lara's."

"Was Coach Murdock involved in this?"

Dr. Crandall wiped his moist brow with a handkerchief. "Absolutely not. He wouldn't have approved. It's not his style. He thought it was his training that turned Billy and the Evanses into musclemen."

"What about Old Man McCarthy?" James asked.

"No. He just filled my prescriptions, no questions asked, like he's been doing for the last twenty years."

James paused. Now came the big question. "What about Nick's murder? Do you know anything about that?"

Dr. Crandall looked James right in the eye. "I know I'm not the most reliable source, given what you've uncovered about me. But I swear to you that I have no earthly idea who killed Nick. I would gladly give up everything that I have before I would make Lara the daughter of a murderer. And I'm still not convinced that Nick's murder is linked to this whole steroids thing. It could just be some maniac out on the loose."

James didn't know whether to believe him or not, but his gut feeling was that Dr. Crandall was telling the truth. "And Billy? Do you have any idea where he is?"

"No, I honestly don't," the doctor said.

They both jumped when the office phone rang. Dr. Crandall turned on the intercom, his hand visibly shaking.

"Yes?"

"There's a young man on the line demanding to speak to you. Should I put him through?" the operator asked.

"Yes, go ahead," the doctor said, picking up the phone. "This is Dr. Crandall. Can I help you?"

James couldn't hear the person on the other end. But suddenly Dr. Crandall frowned and gripped the edge of his desk. His eyes widened and he looked ill. He met James's eyes, then motioned for James to keep quiet as he turned on the speaker phone. He spoke softly but firmly. "Yes, Billy. Of course I remember you. It's good to hear your voice again."

Billy! James could feel his heart start to pound. Billy Owens was alive?

"Did you think I was dead?" Billy asked.

"I didn't know what had happened to you. But I'm glad that you're alive and well."

There was a prolonged silence on the other end of the line. Dr. Crandall looked at James helplessly. "What can I do for you, Billy?" he finally asked.

"I have your daughter," Billy said.

Dr. Crandall closed his eyes and leaned back in his chair. James was concerned by how pale the doctor looked.

"Did you hear me, Doc?" Billy barked.

"Yes," he uttered. "What do you mean, you have Lara?" James put his head down on the desk.

"I'm not going to hurt her, if you cooperate," Billy said.

"What do you want me to do, Billy?" James was amazed at how calmly Dr. Crandall spoke.

"Meet me at the gym at midnight. Bring steroids—lots of them, enough for a long time. And ten thousand dollars in small bills. Can you handle that?"

Dr. Crandall's composure began to crack. "That's less than four hours. The banks and the pharmacies are all closed. . . ."

"That's *your* problem, Doc. You know the time and place. And don't bring the cops, if you ever want to see little Lara again."

"How do I know that you really have her?" the doctor asked weakly.

"You want proof?" James heard Billy instruct Lara to "Say hi to Daddy" as he handed her the phone.

"Daddy?" Lara's voice sounded strained.

"Honey, are you okay?"

"I'm fine. I—" Billy grabbed the phone from Lara's hand and said "That's enough" before slamming it down.

Dr. Crandall turned off the speakerphone. He leaned over his desk and put his head in his hands. The man that James had come to confront had suddenly become his partner in a desperate struggle to save Lara.

Chapter 14

Billy placed his pocketknife down on the kitchen counter. "I won't be needing this anymore."

"What if I try to escape?" Lara asked, trying to sound tough.

"You won't," Billy said, pulling an enormous butcher knife out of a kitchen drawer.

"What are you going to do with that?" Lara asked nervously.

Billy laughed. "Nothing, probably. I need it for a visual aid. Your dad needs to know that I mean business. *This* will let him know," Billy said, brandishing the butcher knife wildly.

Lara stood silently, watching Billy pretend to swordfight his shadow with the butcher knife. He went in for the kill, then threw his hands up in the air in victorious celebration. Suddenly he whirled to face Lara, and she instinctively backed up.

"We've got almost four hours to kill. Why don't you have a seat in the living room? Watch

126

some TV. Maybe you can catch the latest reports of my death," he cackled.

"No, thanks," Lara said quietly.

Billy launched into a manic tirade. "What'sa matter, Lara? Dont'cha like my house? Oh, that's right. You've never been here before, have you? How rude of me not to remember! Shall I give you the grand tour? Where should I begin, with the roach motels or with the mouse-traps?"

"I've been here before," Lara corrected him.

"Oh, yeah? When?"

"Yesterday."

"Is that so? Well, isn't that sweet? Lara waits until Billy's gone, until he's probably *dead*, to come over to his house for a visit."

"I was worried about you," Lara said. "I came over to see if your mother had heard from you."

Billy whirled out of the kitchen and picked up a picture of his mother from the dining-room table. "Ah, dear old Mom," he said devilishly, dancing with the picture in one hand and the knife in the other. "She's always worried about me. She's so concerned about my disappearance that's she's off at work right now slinging hash."

"She thinks you ran away. Besides, she's got to make a living," Lara protested.

"You call this a living?" Billy asked scornfully, waving his hand around his dilapidated sur-roundings. "I'm sure she's heard about my 'death' by now. The police must have notified her about Chris's arrest and their plans to drag the lake for my body. They couldn't have shown my picture on the news if they hadn't. As a budding young journalist, you should know that."

Lara didn't respond. Billy picked up the remote control and tossed it to Lara. "You sure you don't want to watch some TV?"

"Positive," Lara said, throwing it back at him.

Billy smiled dangerously. "You haven't changed a bit since we were little kids, you know that? You're hard to rattle."

"I may not have changed, but you certainly have," Lara said.

"What's that supposed to mean?"

"You figure it out."

"You are a feisty one, aren't you? Well, we've got to keep ourselves entertained somehow. How about if I tell you a story?"

"Fine," Lara said brusquely.

"Have a seat," he said, pointing toward the couch with his knife. Lara didn't budge. He pointed the knife toward her, and she reluctantly sank onto the couch.

Billy cleared his throat. "This story is called 'The Doctor and His Daughter.' Are you ready?"

Lara nodded in dread. Billy pulled a chair in front of her, sat down, and pantomimed he was driving a car. "Once upon a time, a doctor took a vacation with his wife and daughter." Billy put his arm around his imaginary family.

"The doctor's best friend and his family came along for the ride," Billy said. Lara winced.

"Everybody was happy. The doctor's little daughter lay fast asleep, deep in dreamland. The best friend's son slept, too. Isn't this a pretty picture?" he asked innocently.

"No," Lara answered grimly.

Billy grinned. "That's because you know what happens next. WHAM! CRASH! Blood and bright lights all around. Sirens wail. A nightmare comes to life. The doctor and his daughter are fine, but the doctor's wife hasn't exactly been able to keep her head on her shoulders, if you know what I mean."

"Shut up, Billy!" Lara screamed.

"And in the back seat, the doctor's best friend bleeds all over his son. The kid can't stop his father from bleeding. He reaches a hand out to the doctor's daughter, his playmate, his best friend . . ."

Billy reached his hand out to Lara. She sat motionless.

"But she can't help him. She has her own hands full and won't let go of her mother. She just keeps shaking her and shaking her and shaking her until—"

"That's enough, Billy! End of story," Lara practically sobbed, hiding her face in her hands.

"Ah, but that's what you think." Billy put the chair back and sat down next to Lara on the couch. She moved away from him.

"Flash forward ten years. The boy has become a man."

"Spare me the hyperbole," Lara said bitterly.

"But he needs to be big and strong. Bigger and stronger than anyone else. Then he can defeat the enemies who threaten his future. He knows if he takes hormones he'll become invincible. That's what he needs. Who will help this poor boy get them? Maybe a certain doctor he knows?"

Lara knew immediately what Billy was implying. The thought that her father might have supplied Billy with the steroids hadn't crossed her mind. Her father could be a jerk at times, but give out steroids? No way.

"You don't know this part of the story, do you?" Billy taunted her. "The doctor gives the boy the drugs, and the boy shares them with his friends. Everybody's happy—the boy is big and strong, and the doctor feels good for helping the boy."

"I don't believe a word of this garbage," Lara interrupted. "My father had nothing to do with your steroids. You're just saying this to try to upset me."

"You want proof?" Billy asked. "You sound just like your father, asking to hear your voice on the phone. You Crandalls need proof of everything."

"Put up or shut up, Billy. Have you got any proof?"

"Well, no. Not on me," he admitted. "But I'm the one with the knife here. I'm in control. I don't have to prove anything to you. You just have to take my word on it."

"Your word means nothing to me," Lara said.

"Fine. I'm not going to tell you the rest of the story."

"That's because you don't know how the story ends, do you? It's not over yet."

"No, but I'll tell you how it is *going* to end. The boy gets the drugs, takes the doctor's money, and runs away to start his life over again, somewhere else. Somewhere better. Rich and powerful, he conquers the world."

"And what happens to the doctor and his daughter?"

Billy stared at Lara intently and shrugged his shoulders. "Maybe they live and maybe they die. Frankly, Miss Scarlett, I don't give a damn." He laughed insanely, but Lara knew how dead serious he really was.

Billy seemed to have lost his mind completely, but Lara couldn't help thinking about what he had said about her father. Could it be true? Could her father be the source of the steroids? Lara shuddered just thinking it. Would she ever be able to look him in the eye again? Would she even get the chance?

James broke the long silence that had fallen over Dr. Crandall's office after the phone call from Billy. "What should we do? Are you going to call the cops?"

"No way. If Billy thinks I've called the cops, he could hurt Lara. I can't underestimate his threats. Steroids can make a person extremely violent and paranoid. And homicidal."

"So what are you going to do? Give him what he wants?"

Dr. Crandall leaned back in his chair. "No, I can't, even if I wanted to. There's no way to get those drugs or that kind of money at this hour. But Billy won't buy that. He's completely irrational. Besides, I don't want him to keep Lara overnight. There's no telling what he would do to her."

"That doesn't leave us a whole lot of options," James said.

"We've got to get him to free Lara, then trap him. Then we can call the cops. We can't take the chance that they might blow this whole thing by showing up early with their sirens blaring."

"Makes sense to me. But how do we trap him?"

Dr. Crandall pointed at James. "That's where you come in."

"I do?"

"You're my secret weapon. Billy doesn't know that you're working on this story, does he?"

James thought for a moment. "I don't think

so. Lara didn't tell me about it until after Billy disappeared."

"Perfect. Then he won't think anyone else is working against him except me."

James thought Dr. Crandall should act soon. Time was growing short. How were they going to trap Billy? Did Lara's father have a plan, or was he just thinking out loud?

Dr. Crandall continued, "Our other advantage is that we know where the meeting place is going to be. That was Billy's mistake. This gives us time to set up a trap for him there."

James drummed his fingers on the doctor's desk. "Cut to the chase. How do we nab him?"

Dr. Crandall nodded. "Patience. I'll explain it to you. It's a foolproof setup—that is, as long as you pull off your part of it. And believe me, your part couldn't be simpler."

James settled back in his chair. From the sound of things, Lara's life would soon be in his hands.

Chapter 15

James looked nervously at his digital watch. He was crouched beneath the bleachers of the gym. It was 11:59 P.M. Any minute, Billy would arrive with Lara and the exchange would be made. Dr. Crandall stood against the far wall, his black medical bag clutched tightly in his hands.

As the numbers on James's watch flipped to 12:00 midnight, Billy and Lara entered the dimly lit gym. *Right on schedule,* James thought. He could feel his heart beating in his throat.

Lara's hands were tied behind her back, and Billy held a butcher knife to her throat. James could hear Dr. Crandall unconsciously whispering a prayer to himself.

Billy walked a few paces toward halfcourt with Lara in tow. He stopped when he saw that Dr. Crandall was standing still. "Hey, Doc, what'cha got in your magic bag? Any goodies for me?" Billy called, his voice echoing in the rafters.

"You know exactly what I've got in here. You

asked for it," the doctor said in a low, firm tone. James couldn't believe how cool and confident Dr. Crandall sounded—especially considering that the bag was empty.

"Hand it over," Billy commanded.

"Not until you let Lara go."

Billy laughed bitterly. "You Crandalls truly amaze me. Skepticism must run in your family. You don't trust me, do you? You think I *want* to kill Lara?"

"All I want is a fair exchange. Let Lara go, and I'll put the bag down at halfcourt. You'll get to it at the same time I get to Lara. That way no one can try anything funny."

Billy scratched his head with the sharp tip of the knife. "Now let me get this straight. . . ."

"No stalling, Billy! Let Lara go, and you'll get the goods."

James peered through the bleachers anxiously as Billy sliced through the rope around Lara's wrists. She ran over to the bleachers on the far side of the gym. The bait had been taken. The trap was about to be sprung.

As Dr. Crandall walked slowly toward center court, James took out the scalpel the doctor had given him and started cutting the rope attached to the fishing net in the rafters. The timing had to be perfect, so that the net would fall on Billy at the precise moment that he reached the bag.

Dr. Crandall placed the bag down in the middle of the red circle at center court, then turned and walked to Lara. Lara ran to her father with outstretched arms. James sawed feverishly on the rope as Billy raced to the bag.

The rope was down to a small sliver when Billy reached the red circle and bent down to pick up the black bag. His pulse pounding, James worked with the scalpel frantically, but the final strand just wouldn't snap.

Billy picked up the empty bag and knew he had been tricked. James watched as Billy seemed to move in slow motion. He turned and looked at the Crandalls, who were locked in a tearful embrace.

James panicked. He only had a split second left before Billy charged the Crandalls. His hands were shaking badly, and he dropped the scalpel on the floor.

The noise distracted Billy. He looked over at the bleachers where James was hiding. James ducked out of sight, cursing himself under his breath.

Dr. Crandall looked up when he heard the noise. Suddenly, he rushed Lara to the doors that led outside to the parking lot. Billy dropped the bag and sprinted after them. James picked up the scalpel, but it was too late. Billy reached the exit door a half-step before the Crandalls.

"Where do you think you're going?" he snarled viciously as he blocked their escape. They backed away from his knife. "I thought you said there weren't going to be any tricks!"

James gripped the scalpel in frustration. There was nothing that he could do to help Lara and her father. If he ran out from behind the bleachers, Billy would kill one or both of them. And even if he could jump Billy from behind, his small scalpel was no match for Billy's big butcher knife.

As Billy threatened the Crandalls, James tried to analyze the situation calmly. His only advantage over Billy was that Billy hadn't found him yet. If he waited and stayed hidden, an opportunity to trap Billy might present itself again. Billy was making the Crandalls back up across the gym floor; maybe James could drop the net, after all.

"What'sa matter?" Billy yelled. "Afraid I'm going to kill you?"

Lara and her father continued retreating in silent terror.

"You're right!" Billy screamed. The Crandalls shuffled backward through the red circle, and James primed the scalpel to cut the last strand.

"Only not with this," Billy said as he suddenly lunged at them, jumping over the center circle and landing in an exaggerated fencing pose, the tip of the knife perched inches away from Dr. Crandall's throat.

Caught off guard, James missed his chance to drop the net on Billy. The split-second window of opportunity crashed closed once again.

"Keep walking and you'll come to your final

resting place," Billy chuckled. The Crandalls found themselves backed up against the far wall of the gym. Shivering with fear, they stood between the entrances to the steamroom and the weight room, which was still sealed off with yellow tape marked "Crime Scene."

"Here we are!" Billy announced. The Crandalls looked over their shoulders into the weight room. The floor was still stained with Chuck's blood, and the police had drawn a chalk outline where his body had fallen.

"You idiots! I'm not going to kill you two in there! As you can see, the weight room has already been used once today," he said, slashing through the yellow police tape with his knife.

Billy opened the door to the steamroom and forced Lara and her father inside. "Unlike Chuck's quick, sweet demise, yours will be slow, painful—and hot!" he said.

Paralyzed with fear, James watched as Billy slammed shut the door of the steamroom and slapped the combination lock on it. Then Billy adjusted the temperature setting on the wall by the door, turning the knob all the way into the red zone marked "Danger." He pressed his face against the small window on the door and waited for several minutes, gleefully watching the Crandalls squirm from the increasingly brutal heat.

James wanted to rush to their rescue, but his feet felt as if they were frozen to the floor. "Hot enough for you?" Billy taunted them through the glass. "You ain't felt nothin' yet! Wait until I get to the *master* controls in the boiler room! This will feel like Alaska!" Laughing crazily, he tore out of the gym and bounded down the stairs to the basement.

With Billy gone, James ran to the steamroom and tried to jerk open the door. It was no use. The lock was strong, and James didn't know the combination. He swore in frustration as he realized he couldn't break the reinforced glass. But at least he reached over on the wall and turned off the heat inside.

He peered through the steamed-up window. Lara looked out at him, her face transfixed with helpless fear. She knelt next to her father, who was slumped on the floor clutching his left shoulder.

There was nothing that James could do but watch.

"Daddy, are you okay?" Lara cried, shaking him gently.

Dr. Crandall's eyes were closed tightly. His face was bright red, screwed up in a wince of pain. Slowly he opened his eyes to look up at his daughter. In a weak voice, he said, "I'm sorry."

Lara felt involuntary tears begin to course down her cheeks. She held her father more tightly and noticed that his breathing was labored and irregular.

"Don't be silly, Daddy. Everything's going to be okay."

Dr. Crandall grimaced in a pathetic imitation of a smile, then Lara felt his body go limp.

"Daddy! Daddy!" Lara shook his shoulders slightly and patted his flushed cheek.

"Daddy, wake up! We have to get out of here!"

But there was no response. Lara's heart seemed to freeze over. She stared up through the window at James with a horrified expression on her face. His eyes were open wide as he watched helplessly. Lara shifted her position so she could put her head to her father's chest. She listened with all her might, but there was no heartbeat. He was dead.

"Oh, my God!" Lara scrambled backward away from her father's body, then reached back and grabbed his hand.

"Daddy—not yet—please—" She broke down into a paroxysm of sobs. But the hiss of steam beginning to escape from the pipes again brought her head up. Billy must have gotten down into the boiler room. Lara was going to die, too.

"Oh, Daddy, please forgive me." *It was all for nothing,* she thought—Nick's death, Chuck Evans's, and now her own father's. *For nothing.*

Or was it? With a new will, Lara got unsteadily to her feet. It was already becoming stiflingly hot with the new steam.

Looking around the cramped room, she noticed that one of the ceiling panels was dislodged. Could this be a way out? Lara lay her father's head gently on the floor and closed his eyes, which were frozen in a stare. She stepped on a bench against the wall and removed the panel.

Looking inside, she saw that the crawl space above the steamroom went above the adjacent hallway. Before wriggling into the hot, dark space, she motioned for James to go out into the hallway. She would need his help to get down from the ceiling.

Lara looked back at her father lying motionless on the floor and wiped the tears from her eyes. After a couple of aborted tries, she managed to pull herself up into the claustrophobic metal tunnel. She crept along slowly on her hands and knees, trying to avoid the soft dead center of the panels. When she knew she had crawled past the steamroom, she lifted one of the panels above the hallway. Looking down, she saw James standing under her, ready to catch her as soon as she jumped.

She closed her eyes and fell swiftly into his arms.

"Oh, James. My father's dead!"

"Ssh, ssh. It'll be okay. Let's get out of here." Lara leaned against James's chest and clung to him tightly. For a brief moment, she forgot that Billy was still on the loose.

Reality came rushing back when she heard Billy's heavy footsteps coming upstairs from the basement. "Quick, get back under the bleachers," she told James. "My father whispered the plan to me."

James hid once more. Lara, her adrenaline pumping and her emotions rushing, raced to center court and planted herself on the magic red spot. When Billy came back into the gym, he ran to the steamroom window and pressed his face against it.

He jumped back when he saw that only Dr. Crandall was inside. "What the . . ."

"Hey!" Lara called out shakily from her position.

Billy spun around and looked at Lara. Letting out a beastly battle cry, he charged with the butcher knife poised to kill. James knew this would be his last chance to make the trap work. He'd messed it up twice—and the third strike could be deadly.

Lara stood perfectly still, holding her breath as Billy closed in on her. The scalpel sliced cleanly through the last strand of rope, and the fishing net flew down from the rafters. At the last second, Lara threw herself out of the circle and the net fell in a heap on top of Billy.

Screaming hoarsely, Billy struggled to untangle himself. James wound the rope around a pole and yanked hard, lifting Billy off the ground inside the net. With all his strength,

James pulled on the rope until Billy was suspended next to the state championship banner in the rafters, shrieking incomprehensibly. Then James tied the end of the rope to a post supporting the bleachers and ran out to Lara at midcourt.

"Let me down!" Billy screamed.

"Quick!" James exclaimed as he helped Lara up off the gym floor. "Let's go call the cops!"

Lara looked up at Billy, flailing in the net like a fly trapped in a spider's web, and then at James, who stood above her. She had finally completed her steroids investigation, at the cost of several human lives, including her own father's. She didn't feel like much of a heroine.

Lara sat down at the dining-room table and rolled the piece of paper into the typewriter. She could procrastinate no longer. Her father's funeral was tomorrow, but the application for Columbia had to be mailed by midnight tonight. In the confusion and excitement of the steroids scandal, she had put off the essay until the very last moment.

She stared at the question again: "What has been your most significant life experience?" Laughing through her tears, she said, "Here goes nothing," and started pecking away at the keys.

She wrote off the top of her head—no outline,

no editing, no consultation of dictionaries or thesauruses. There was no time for that.

"My most significant life experience ended last night," Lara's essay began, "with the death of my father. He was trying to save my life. We had both become involved with steroids. Neither of us took them. Dad prescribed them. I investigated."

Lara poured her innermost feelings out onto the page. She explained the case in all of its intricate details. She wrote about the accident that had shattered two families' lives, and how the guilt and pain that it had caused came back to haunt them ten years later. She attached page after page of white typing paper as the essay grew longer. This wasn't just for Columbia. Lara was writing this essay for herself as well.

"I thought I knew what being a reporter was all about," Lara wrote in her final paragraph. "I had no idea how painful and difficult it can be, and how much responsibility it can entail. When I started investigating steroids at Cresswell, I thought I had stumbled upon the story of my life. The truth of it was, I really had."

Lara rolled the piece of paper out of the typewriter and turned off the machine. She put the pages in order, attached them to the rest of the application, and sealed the envelope. There was no time to go back and read over what she had written. She would have to drive across town to the twenty-four-hour post office, and it was almost midnight.

She grabbed her keys off the table and ran out to her car. She turned the ignition key several times, but the car wouldn't start. The battery was dead. Lara banged her hands against the steering wheel, then stared at her father's car parked in front of the house. He had never found time to teach her how to use the stick shift. She felt as if she was about to cry, but held back the tears fiercely. If she couldn't deal with this minor dilemma without her father, how could she hope to face the rest of her life without him?

Lara went inside and trudged slowly upstairs to her bedroom. She would have to mail the application a day late. Big deal. Columbia probably wouldn't want her anyway, after the essay she'd written. If anything, they would probably recommend that she see a shrink—just as her father always did.

She put the envelope on the table by her bed and got under the covers. She was all alone. Friends and relatives had offered to come and stay with Lara, but she had turned them all down. She preferred it this way. She was eighteen, an adult, after all.

Lara lay awake, staring at her clock as the numbers slowly flipped to 12:00. She wondered if she would have her nightmares again. If she did, how would she deal with them without her father to comfort her? Would they get worse now that he was gone?

Soon she was asleep. The nightmares never came.

Chapter 16

Lara walked home from school with James, as she had almost every day that spring. She still had her car, but on such beautiful days it was much nicer to walk hand-in-hand.

They reached the door of her house, and Lara peeked into her mailbox. Inside was a thick envelope postmarked "New York, NY." The return address read "Columbia University." Lara snatched it out of the box, stared at it, then dragged James inside the house with her.

They plopped down on the couch. She handed James the envelope. "You read it!"

"Why me?"

"I can't bear it," Lara said, covering her head with a pillow.

James kissed the top of her head and ripped open the envelope. Clearing his throat, he read silently, then out loud. "Congratulations . . ."

Lara shrieked joyously and grabbed James around the neck. He dropped the envelope and lifted her into the air, swinging her around. A note fell out of the envelope, and Lara disengaged herself and picked it up.

"It's a personal note from the dean of the journalism school," she said breathlessly. " 'I have read your remarkable essay and encourage you to enter the undergraduate journalism program. You have the makings of a great reporter.' "

James smiled at Lara. "And all this time you've been afraid that they would reject you because of that essay."

"I know. Can you believe it?"

"You're off to the Big Apple. . . ." James said.

Lara's enthusiasm tapered off. "And scared to death of it. I guess I'll have to take a trip there soon and see what I've gotten myself into."

"It's a very big city. . . ." James said.

"And very far away," Lara finished his thought. She squeezed his hand. "I'm going to miss you so much. Have you come any closer to deciding where you're going?"

"Well, I got accepted into another school yesterday," James said meekly.

"Why didn't you tell me?" Lara asked. "Which one?"

"Oh . . . Columbia," James said, breaking into a smirk.

Lara couldn't believe her ears. "Are you serious? You never even told me you applied!"

"I wasn't going to go unless we both got accepted," James explained. "I wouldn't want to go off to New York City all by myself!"

"What if I had gotten accepted and you hadn't?" Lara asked.

"Gee, I hadn't considered that possibility," James joked.

"You jerk, you've been holding out on me! How come you got your letter yesterday, and mine didn't come until today?"

"I didn't send my application in a day late!" James laughed.

"What did you write your essay on?" Lara needled him.

James put his hand over his heart. "My days as a Cub Scout. It was quite moving, really."

"Did you get a personal note from the dean?"

"Are you kidding? They misspelled my name on the envelope."

"Four more years of you?" Lara teased him. "I don't know if I can stand it!"

"Well, there are always vacations," James reminded her. "Except I guess we'll both be coming back here to Cresswell. Ha! You're stuck with me!"

"Don't be so sure," Lara said, suddenly melancholy.

"What are you talking about?"

"There are too many memories for me to come back here. I've decided that once I go off to college, I'm not coming back. At least not for a while."

"What about the house? Are you going to leave it behind?"

Lara shook her head. "I've arranged with my father's lawyer to have the deed to the house transferred over to Billy's mother. She's stuck here in Cresswell without a family, and I can't help but feel partially responsible. This is all I can do to try to make it up to her."

"You already gave her your dad's car!"

"Her car was falling apart, and I don't need two. Besides, she'll need it to visit Billy in jail. And now when he gets out, he'll have a nice house to come back to."

James shook his head in disbelief. "You're being pretty nice to Billy, considering what he did to your father."

"My father's gone, but Billy is still alive. With his mother's support, he might be able to turn his life around. Now that's he's off the steroids, maybe he can get an education in jail and start over when he gets out. I never want to see Billy again, but that doesn't mean I want him to rot in prison for the rest of his life."

"You're never coming back to Cresswell. I guess I'm not the only one who's been holding out on some big news," James said.

"I was going to tell you about this sooner, but I was afraid you might be hurt. If you went off to another college, I might not have been able to see you again if I didn't come back here."

"Gosh, that's a cheery thought."

"Can't you see?" Lara said, taking hold of James's hand. "There's nothing left for me here. You still have your family to come home to at Thanksgiving and Christmas. All I have is this empty house."

"You could stay at my house. My parents wouldn't mind. They like you, and they hardly ever bite," James said, a hopeful smile returning to his face.

"That's not the point, James," Lara said gently.

"Mom makes a mean turkey!" James said, tickling her softly.

"James, cut it out!" Lara laughed. She squirmed away from him. From across the couch, she opened her eyes wide and looked at him. He had that big dopey grin on his face that drove Lara crazy. "We'll just have to see," she said with a glint in her eye as she leaned over to kiss him.